THE BLESSED COAT

A WORK OF HISTORICAL FICTION BASED ON
ACTUAL EVENTS IN HISTORY THAT
ILLUSTRATES HOW FAR-REACHING OUR ACTS
OF KINDNESS CAN BE

B. E. CLEGG

D1489911

GCS
Distributing

CONTENTS

1. The Coat   1
2. Brent   7
3. Fredrick   22
4. Ernst   36
5. Viktor   53
6. Kurt   86
7. Thomas Grey   96
8. Ed and Joanie   113

Author's Notes   145
Acknowledgments   151
Bibliography   153
About the Author   155

CHAPTER 1

THE COAT

A SLENDER MAN with a well-groomed beard walked slowly through the streets of Salt Lake City. His head down, he was just looking at where he was walking, deep in thought. It was a cold winter morning and the wind cut through him. He had a lot on his mind with many problems weighing heavily on his shoulders. He had been President of the Church of Jesus Christ of Latter-Day Saints for just a few months. World War II had ended in Europe in May and in the Pacific in August. Everyone was so grateful to have the war finally over.

Winter now covered the land with dark skies, cold temperatures and snow. His thoughts were about the members of the church in Europe and the other people of Europe in general. The reports he had gotten back were of a people who were ragged, dirty, poor, cold and starving.

These people, he was told, were in need of everything. He wanted to do more.

He had made an appointment with President Harry S. Truman to ask for help getting needed supplies to the people in the war torn countries. President Truman had asked him why he wanted to send anything to Europe, adding, "their money isn't any good."

"We don't want *their* money," the man said, "We want to give it to them."

President Truman asked him when he could have things ready.

"We're ready now," the man said.

After thinking about it for a minute President Truman approved transportation.

A few small packages had already been sent and gotten through. The reports coming back were of gratitude for the much needed clothes, canned goods and soap. But it was only a drop in the bucket to what was needed.

After the word was out that the government and Red Cross would help move the donations, people started giving more and more to the welfare storehouse of the church. They not only gave clothes and bedding, but also canned goods, writing paper, shampoo, soap, shoes, tooth paste, tooth brushes, bandages, vitamins, hats, coats and toys. Many people also donated cans of shortening and lard after hearing that the people in Europe were in desperate need of fat in their diet. Any grease or fat had been earmarked, in the last six years, to make munitions.

The man was pleased this morning as he thought of yesterday's meeting. The logistics of getting the packages of needed items to the designated places seemed to be going well. He took a deep breath of cold air and looked up from where he was walking.

He saw a group of men clearing the ice from the gutters along the streets so that the storm drains would be open. As he watched them work, he noticed one of the workers had only a light sweater on. As he got closer he could see the man was shivering.

When he reached the man, he stopped and said, "It's too cold to be working in just a sweater, where's your coat?"

The worker said, "I don't have one."

The tall man smiled, unbuttoned his coat, removed it and handed it to the worker and said, "This is a good wool coat, it will keep you warm."

The worker looked at him in surprise and said, "I can't take your coat."

"I work just across the street there and I can walk over there with no coat. Please take the coat."

With a grateful nod, the offering was accepted.

As the tall man walked across the street he smiled as he heard the street cleanup worker ask who he was. Another man said, "That's President George Albert Smith."

President Smith reached for the door of the church office building, and glanced back at the men working on the ice. He saw the man still watching him, holding the coat tightly to his chest. He silently prayed that all that would come in contact with the coat would feel God's love for them and be blessed with what they were in need of, and they would feel comfort and peace. He turned, opened the door and walked in out of sight.

LUCY SMITH WAS JUST FINISHING up making supper when she heard the door open and close. She glanced around the corner to see her husband standing in the front room looking very chilled. "Where's your coat?" she asked him.

"I gave it to someone that needed it more than I did."

"Well, come into the kitchen and stand by the stove and get warm. Supper is almost ready."

He stood by the stove for a few minutes then sat down at the table and watched Lucy put the last few dishes of food on the table.

"Do we still have that old brown coat that I wore a few years ago?" he asked.

She sat down across from him. "Yes I think it's in a box in the back of the closet." She reached over and took his hand. "Your hand is still cold." Then with a smile she said, "I'll find your coat for you after supper." She gave his hand a squeeze. "Try to hang on to this coat, okay?" she said with a smile and winked. He smiled back and nodded. Then they bowed their heads to give thanks for a warm home and good food to eat.

CHAPTER 2

BRENT

BRENT WATCHED the man walk to the office building, briefly stop and look back, then go in. He put on the coat and wrapped it around him and buttoned it up. It was a little tight on him but snug and warm. He went back to work with the other men on his team of temporary workers.

At day's end the temporary workers received their pay. One by one, their names were called and they were given their pay for that day. Everyone's name was called except his and he wondered why. After all the other temporary workers were paid and gone, the foreman turned to Brent. "Mr. Cox, I'd like to talk to you if you have a few minutes."

"Sure," said Brent. They sat down on a

nearby bench and the foreman asked him if he was interested in a full-time job. Brent was surprised.

BRENT HAD JOINED the army when he turned 18. He'd been assigned to the 82nd Airborne. He'd made several jumps and seen much of the terrors of war.

But then came the jump into Holland in September of 1944. As experienced as Brent was, when he landed he broke his leg just above the ankle and cracked three ribs. He was in the middle of a major fire fight and was in unbelievable pain. Adrenalin was the only thing that kept him moving.

Brent pulled himself into some bushes and kept his head down. He hoped someone from his squad would come along to help him. The battle roared on most of the night but slowly started to move away from him.

When morning came and things were quiet, he found himself drifting in and out of a pain filled fog. He woke up once long enough to realize that someone was talking to him and trying to move him. He couldn't understand what they were saying and every time they moved him he blacked out again.

When Brent became aware again, he found himself in a barn or shed of some kind with a splint on his leg. Someone was trying to make him drink some water.

He drank what he could get down and then looked up to see two older women and a boy about seven or eight years old looking down at him. They smiled and said something he didn't understand, then offered him a cup of warm milk.

One lady turned to the boy and said something. The young boy spun around and ran off. The milk tasted good and Brent slowly drank the whole cup. He laid his head back and drifted off to sleep again. He woke to the sound of men talking. Two Army medics were following the boy into the barn. They kneeled down beside Brent and looked at his leg.

"We are going to have to do something about this," one of the medics said.

"Better give him some morphine before we start working on it," the other one said. He reached for his bag and pulled out a syringe and filled it full of some medication and then turned to Brent. "We are going to give you something for your pain and then reset your leg. We'll splint it again but after that we are going to have to leave you here. We'll radio back to our unit and tell them where you are. They'll come looking for you in a day or two. We have many who are in worse shape than you and we need to tend to them first. You have someone here who will take care of you and keep you safe for a few days."

Brent felt a pin prick in his arm and felt himself drifting into a drugged sleep. When he again became aware of where he was, his leg was really hurting and he could hardly breathe because of his broken ribs. He tried to sit up a little, but that just made it worse. When he tried to lie back down, he yelled out in pain which brought the young boy running in. He said something to Brent and then disappeared. In a few moments, the two women came hustling in. One had a bowl with some kind of broth in it that she began spooning into Brent's mouth. It tasted good and he tried his best to enjoy it in spite of his pain.

The young boy came back with a blanket

and a bowl of warm water and some rags. They helped him remove his coat and roll up his shirt sleeves. They gave him a small bar of soap and he washed his face, arms and hands. It felt good. As he laid back down he winced. One of the women pulled a syringe out of her pocket, walked over to Brent and stuck it into his arm. He soon felt the sweet relief of sleep overtaking him again.

What he remembered next was being wrapped up tight in a blanket and hearing lots of talking. He noticed the sound of trucks driving around outside the barn. Then three American GIs walked in and asked him how he was doing. They told him not to worry, they were going to get him out of there and back to the Medical Evac unit.

Brent tried to sit up but let out a yelp as he did so. "We have something to give you for that too," said one of the men. Two more men came in with a stretcher. They got him on it and carried him outside and onto a truck that had four other wounded soldiers on it. They were all hooked up to IVs and seemed unaware of anything going on around them.

A medic came into the back of the truck

and started an IV on Brent, shot some meds into it and told him he'd been lucky that the Dutch family had found him and hid him from the Germans. "You owe them your life. If the Germans had found you they would have shot you." Then he left.

Brent remembered as the truck started moving, he heard the sound of the glass IV bottle clanging against the side wall of the truck. Then once again, he fell into a deep sleep away from the pain.

When he opened his eyes again, he found he was in a bed with clean white sheets and his ribs had been wrapped up tight. His leg was tied up to a support above his bed. He asked the nurse where he was. She told him he was on a hospital ship headed back to the states.

"Home!" he thought. "I'm going home."

Brent spent four weeks in a hospital in Maryland and then was discharged, given his last paycheck and a train ticket to Salt Lake City, UT. He was still on crutches but could get around okay. He enjoyed his ride home. Looking out the window he was struck with the beauty of the land as it floated by. No blown up buildings or homes. No big holes in the farm land where a bomb had hit. No military trucks full of young men weighed down with guns and grenades. No shabby looking people with blank looks in their eyes.

Looks of fear, desperation and hopelessness were about all he had seen in the last two and a half years. He saw none of that as he looked out his window. How grateful he was to be back in the States.

"We are truly blessed in this country," he thought as he drifted off to sleep.

Salt Lake wasn't home but close. That's where the jobs were so that's where he stayed. He found himself a small room to rent in the back of a home and worked at odd jobs. He found a small group of friends and spent his evenings healing and reading books he picked up from the library. When his leg could finally hold him up without pain and his ribs didn't hurt anymore, he was grateful.

Since Brent was now feeling stronger, one of his friends set him up on a blind date. "She's from Holland and I told her a little about what happened to you when you jumped into Holland. She was interested in talking to you."

That was how Brent met Elsa.

She and her mother were sent to Iceland by her father in 1939 just after Hitler invaded Poland. Her father seemed to know Hitler wasn't going to stop there so he got the two women he cared about out of the country with a promise he would join them as soon as he could. They never heard from him again.

Elsa hoped with the end of the war that they would find him. But they had heard nothing in the last few months.

On their first meeting Elsa peppered Brent with questions about his time in Holland. When was he there, where did he land, what town was he near, what was the name of the people who took him in, would he like to go back for a visit? She was so thrilled to talk to someone that had been in Holland recently.

Brent's experience on their first meeting was quite different. Elsa was a strikingly beautiful woman, the kind of woman that turned heads when she walked down the street. When Brent first saw her it took his breath away. He sat quietly and answered all of Elsa's questions but he had to remind himself to breathe. After a few more dates he found that she was just as beautiful on the inside as she was on the outside. She was smart, kind and compassionate.

After a few more months of dating, at an afternoon lunch of pasta, on a whim, he asked her to marry him. She looked at him for what seemed like a long time then grinned. The smile lit up her whole face, the small restaurant they were in and Brent's life.

"I think I would like that," she said as her smile got bigger.

After they were married, they moved into a small apartment. Together they were very happy. They both worked, he at odd jobs that he could find, she at ZCMI department store. That gave them just enough income to subsist nicely.

Then, as in all people's lives, the challenges began to come their way. Elsa became pregnant and it wasn't an easy pregnancy. In the last few months she had to quit work and stay off her feet. After the baby girl was born Elsa still wasn't very strong and it took her two months to feel even half-way well again.

In the meantime with just Brent's income, it was becoming harder and harder to keep food on the table and pay the bills. Brent sold anything he had that he could get money out of.

To top it off, their baby became sick and they didn't have any money to take her to a doctor.

So when Brent's foreman asked to talk with him after the other temporary employees received their paychecks, he was scared that the job he had been doing was over. Instead, he was offered a full time job. Brent just about yelled with joy.

"Yes," he said, "I would love a full time job."

The foreman handed him his check for the day's work and told him what his new wages would be. He asked him if that would be okay.

Brent had to keep from smiling as he answered, "Yes, that will be fine."

"We'll talk about what we want you to do tomorrow morning. See you then." The foreman stood and shook Brent's hand and walked down the street. Brent sat on the bench for a few minutes to reflect on the blessings of that day. It was a cold evening but the coat he'd been given was warm. He finally stood, pulled the coat more closely around him, and walked home.

Brent opened his apartment door carefully, knowing that the baby and Elsa might be asleep. As he stepped inside, sure enough both were asleep on the couch.

He loved seeing them sleeping. They looked so peaceful with the baby wrapped in her pink blanket and Elsa with a smile on her face.

Elsa looked cold with no blanket over her, so he took off his coat and carefully covered them both with it before heading for the bathroom to get cleaned up.

The next morning, Elsa had hundreds of questions about the coat and the new job. He answered all of them and told the story of how he got the coat.

"And," he said, "here is my paycheck from yesterday. I want you to take the baby to a doctor tomorrow and get some medicine. If there is any money left, get some groceries for a nice dinner. We need to celebrate."

The next few weeks were spent learning a new job, getting used to a new boss and

making new friends. Each night as Brent returned home, his wife and baby seemed hap-
pier and healthier. He became more relaxed
and started enjoying life more.

One evening when he returned home
Elsa noticed he had a rip in one of the
sleeves of his coat. He hadn't even noticed it
and had no idea how or when it happened.

"It's okay, I'll mend it," Elsa said. She
handed him the baby and went to find her
sewing basket. It wasn't long before she had
sewn the V-shaped tear closed.

Brent smiled when he looked at what she
had done. Beautifully even, tight stitches,
sewn with light brown thread that stood out
on the black coat.

"I'm sorry about the color," said Elsa. "It's
the only color I had besides pink or green."

Brent thought it looked like a small military stripe. "Well, it looks good to me. Only I
wish you would have given me a higher
rank." They both laughed.

"Oh by the way, a package came today for
you. It's on the table," said Elsa.

Brent walked to the kitchen table and
pulled open the top of the box. Inside were
shirts, pants, two coats, and a suit. He picked

up the note that lay on the top of the shirts, opened it and began reading.

"The clothes are from a friend's mother," Brent said. "She says Tim has gotten too heavy for them. He told her to send them to me because he remembered that we were the same size. She says that she hopes they fit."

He pulled out the suit and tried on the jacket. It fit pretty well. Then he pulled out the coats. One was a top coat, to wear with the suit. The other was a heavy work coat.

"This is great! I'll have a nice coat and a great work coat and they fit me perfectly. As much as I appreciate the coat I was given by President Smith, it has always been a little small on me."

"What are you going to do with that one now you have two new ones?" Elsa asked.

"I don't know. Maybe I'll donate it to the things that are being collected to be sent to Europe."

"That's a good idea." Elsa said.

~

BRENT WALKED down the same street he had cleaned up yesterday. The black, woolen coat hung over his arm. When he got to the donation center, he stepped off to one side of the big door and bowed his head.

"Dear God," he prayed silently. "I just want to say thanks for this coat. It has blessed me in many ways. It kept me warm today so I could work in the cold weather and give my employer a good full day's labor. Because I could give a full day's work, I now have a full time, permanent job. It gave me hope. With all the horrors that I have seen and heard about in the last few years it was wonderful to know that there are some people who still feel compassion for others.

"Today it is going to give me the opportunity to give back the kindness that was given to me. I pray this coat will bring warmth and comfort to someone in much worse circumstances than me."

As Brent raised his head and opened his eyes, he saw a young girl staring at him.

"Can I help you?" she asked.

"Yes, I'd like to donate this coat to the winter clothes being sent to Europe." He ran his finger over the stitches on the sleeve one last time and handed the girl the coat. He then turned and walked toward home.

The coat was cleaned, gently folded, and placed with other warm clothes in a large wooden crate. The crate was closed up tight, placed on a truck and driven to the train station where it would start its journey to its final destination.

CHAPTER 3

FREDRICK

FREDRICK WALKED SLOWLY down the dirt road. The fields on both sides of him were covered with a light dusting of snow hiding the green pastures underneath.

He pulled his coat tighter around him and smiled as he thought about the last few weeks. He and his family had gone to a meeting of church members at which a large crate of clothes were distributed to the people who needed them for the upcoming winter. How grateful he was to get a new pair of pants, a heavy wool sweater and the long black coat he had on. They were the first "new" clothes they had gotten in five years.

Fredrick's wife and girls had gotten new dresses and warm socks. They were all very pleased. They were also given some food, mostly canned things, but they were happy with anything. They also got some fresh fruit along with onions, carrots and potatoes.

LIFE since 1938 had been hard. Fredrick ran a small farm in Germany where he raised vegetables, cows and his children. He sold cheese and vegetables to the local restaurants and at markets in town. He loved making cheese, so he was trying to increase his herd when Hitler changed everything.

Fredrick didn't think his small farm would be something the country would be interested in. He was wrong. "All things were to be done for the "Fatherland." Everything he and his family produced became the property of Germany. The government would tell Fredrick and his family how much of what they produced they could keep for themselves.

In the beginning, Hitler's ideas sounded good. He talked of wholesome values and the importance of family. But, it wasn't long before all that changed. Fredrick had to lie about how much he manufactured and steal his own produce to feed his family. He smuggled milk, bread and cheese down the road to his friends. He said Hitler turned him into a liar, a smuggler and a thief.

FREDRICK HAD a good friend named Isaac. They grew up together, went to school together, studied, worked, played, and dreamed together. They married and started families at the same time. Isaac came to Fredrick's Christian wedding and Fredrick stood up for Isaac at his Jewish wedding. Isaac moved into a home just a mile and a half down the road from Fredrick. After Hitler passed a law that Jews could no longer have a job or buy anything, Fredrick started making late night trips to Isaac's home with food. He couldn't stand the thoughts of his two little boys going without milk and something to eat. So late at night, or early in the morning, Fredrick would sneak down to Isaac's house with a gallon of milk, loaves of bread and some cheese and talk to Isaac for a while.

It was always a challenge visiting late at night at Isaac's home. Isaac's wife Ruth was not a good housekeeper. And now that the boys couldn't go to school, Ruth had taken on the challenge to educate them. With the light of just one candle, Fredrick often would trip over all the projects that Ruth and the boys were doing.

She loved science. She would take her boys on long walks in the woods and talk about biology and all kinds of nature sciences from how things grow, moss on trees, to how rocks were formed. The remnants of each lesson were brought home and left on the floor.

So when Fredrick arrived in the middle of the night with little light it was a challenge to navigate the pieces of wood, papers with leafs and flowers stuck on them, jars with all kinds of insects or worms and frogs in them and the rocks that had been built into walls to keep one young man's armies from invading the other's territory.

One night Fredrick knocked on the door several times, but there was no answer and there were no lights visible. When he opened the door, no one was there. He quietly returned home. He went back the next night and found the same thing. On the third night he opened the door and went in. He felt his way to the table and lit one candle.

The house was empty, dark *and clean*. The dishes and laundry were washed and put away, the beds were made, and the floors were swept and clean. There was no one there.

Fredrick asked around in the village about his friends but no one seemed to know anything about them. He did find out that there had been no soldiers of any kind in or around their village in the last three weeks. This gave him hope that they had not been arrested, but just quietly slipped away. He never did find out what happened to them, but deep down he knew he would never see them again. Long after the war ended, their disappearance still troubled him. They were good friends and he missed them.

~

WHEN THE WAR ENDED, things on Fredrick's farm slowly returned to normal. Caring for his family and his small herd of dairy cows kept him occupied.

On a cold, autumn evening, Fredrick searched the pastures for one of his missing cows. She was due to give birth any day. He found her just before she gave birth to a healthy heifer.

Her sides still heaved and Fredrick realized she wasn't done. Another calf was coming. The mama cow struggled and strained until finally, Fredrick had to pull the second calf out.

Afterwards, the cow began to shiver and tremble as if she was going into shock. Fredrick took off his coat and laid it over the cow to warm her up. He talked to her and held her head, terrified he was going to lose her.

"Come on girl, you have to live! Your babies will die if you don't. Without you I have no way to feed them. Please hang on!"

After a full half hour of shaking, she stopped quivering, stood up and started licking and nursing her calves.

Fredrick was relieved. He'd had so many blessings in the last few weeks including extra food, finding his cow, two new calves and new warm clothes for him and his family just when they needed them. He picked up his coat, shook the straw from it, put it on and left for his meeting.

He was on his way to a church get-together at what was left of the old building they used to meet in. It had one side of it blown away by a bomb blast, but most of it was still standing. One big room and one smaller room were in relatively good shape. The big room was used for meeting together, cooking and distributing the survival items that were coming from America.

The smaller room had been turned into a bathing room. While they were cooking food, water was also being heated up for baths. Due to the scarcity of fuel, it was still against the law to use fuel to heat water for a bath. Here, water was heated at the same time and place as the cooking.

People could come and meet together openly for the first time in years. They were fed physically and spiritually. They were allowed to clean up, were given clean clothes and sent home with food, blankets, soap and renewed faith that life was finally going to improve.

Fredrick loved the feeling of helping. As he walked he let out a long sigh. It was as if it was cleansing him of all the struggles and worries of the last few years. His spirits seem to soar as he thought about the good things to come.

Evening turned into night as he came in sight of the meeting house. He could see lights and people moving around and talking. It made him smile.

Then he saw a figure standing in the dark

about fifty feet ahead of him. He was watching everything that was going on. He was not too far from Fredrick but the figure hadn't seen or heard him coming.

People these days were skittish. Fredrick didn't know what he would do when he made himself known, and he didn't want to surprise him. He started walking again, but this time he also began whistling so the man could heard him coming.

The young man whirled around when he realized that someone was coming up behind him.

"Hey, didn't mean to surprise you," said Fredrick. "I didn't even see you there." He introduced himself and reached out his hand to shake.

The young man gripped his hand, "My name is Ernst. I'm on my way to my grandfather's farm. I've been walking a long time and was surprised to see so many people together down there."

"Well those people are my people and we'd be happy to have you join us if you'd like. I'm betting you're hungry and tired and you look a little cold. I can help you with those things." Fredrick unbuttoned his coat, slipped it off and helped Ernst put it on. Ernst shrugged, shivered a little, slipped into the coat and followed the man to the noisy group. Fredrick introduced him to everyone and then invited him to eat with them.

As Ernst was eating his bowl of stew he looked around. He saw older men bringing wood for the fire and visiting. Women were making bread and stew, laughing as they talked with each other. There was one older gray-haired lady sitting on a chair with many small children on the floor at her feet. She was telling them a story of some kind and the children were spellbound. In the far corner, a young mother sang to her baby as she rocked him to sleep.

The food was good, the people were kind and it felt warm and safe here. It was the first time in many months he felt safe in a group of people.

Ernst was just finishing up his third bowl of stew when Fredrick came over to him. "It's your turn," he said.

"For what?" Ernst asked.

"To get cleaned up," he said. "I'm betting you haven't had a bath in quite some time. We have buckets of hot water and soap and a room to use them in." Then he held out a clean pair of pants, a shirt, and some under-wear. "I hope these fit. Follow me."

Ernst followed Fredrick to a small room. He noticed it contained only a bench against the wall and a drain in the middle of the floor, two buckets of hot water, a small towel and a bar of soap.

Ernst walked in, closed the door and en-joyed soap and warm water and clean clothes for the first time in over a year. It was wonderful.

After he emerged from the "bathing room," Fredrick handed him a blanket. "Some people live close enough to go home after visiting. But some of us stay here overnight and leave in the morning. Find a corner to sleep in."

Ernst looked around and saw people making beds in various places on the floor. That arrangement made him uncomfortable, so he stepped outside. Next to the building, he saw a large, cast iron tub. It sat on its side next to the wall of the building. When he walked over to it and put his hand on it, it was warm. He noticed that the tub was sit-ting right up against the stone wall. On the other side of the wall was the stove that had been used for cooking all night. The stove had heated up the stone wall which in turn had heated up the tub.

"Perfect!" he thought as he climbed in. The tub was hard but warm. As rain started to lightly fall, he noticed it was going to be dry as well.

"Couldn't be better," he thought as he dozed off. "I'm full for the first time in days. I am clean and have new clothes. What a great day!"

Ernst awoke the next morning feeling rested, warm and dry. He found people inside eating warm bread with butter and drinking milk. He hadn't had milk in over a year.

After he finished eating, he stood and announced that he was going to be on his way. He took off the blanket and gave it back to Fredrick.

"How far do you have to go?" said Fredrick.

"Not too far. I should be there in a few days—a week or so at the most." He took the coat off to give it back to Fredrick.

"I want you to have the coat," Fredrick said. "It has brought me luck and blessed me and I pray it will bring good luck to you as well."

"I don't want to take your coat. I'll make it just fine."

"It's cold and you'll need it. Please put it on." Fredrick held it up so Ernst could slip back into it. Gratefully, Ernst did.

"Here are a few things to eat on your journey." Fredrick handed Ernst a can of something he'd never seen before, two apples, ten small potatoes and three onions and a half dozen carrots'. Fredrick also gave him two chicken drumsticks wrapped in paper. "They're cooked and ready to eat," Fredrick told him.

Ernst quickly put the food in the coat pockets and reached his hand out in thanks to Fredrick. Fredrick shook his hand, wished him well and watched him as he walked out of the building. "May God bless and keep you safe."

CHAPTER 4

ERNST

ERNST WAS BORN in Germany but his father got a job in Warsaw Poland, so the family moved. He grew up there in luxury and learned to speak German, Polish, French and some English. He was a good student and had his sights set on a higher education. He got in three semesters of college before Germany invaded Poland.

A few months later, three German officers came to their house and told Ernst's father that he needed to serve in the army of the Third Reich. His father left with the officers that day. The family never heard anything more from or about him after the day he left. It was a year later that German officers came for Ernst.

Because he spoke four languages, Ernst was assigned to an army intelligence group that looked for espionage and sabotage in the area he was stationed. He found and identified spies and spy rings operating in the area. He loved doing what he was assigned to do and was good at it. He received several promotions and was put in charge of his local unit. He felt he was doing a great service for his county.

Each morning, Ernst would go over a list of spies that had been identified and taken in for questioning. He would go over the record of interrogations.

One morning he saw the names of four people he recognized from Warsaw. They were two older couples that he remembered as kind gentle people. As he read, he found that these old people had been tortured. All of their possessions were taken from them and they were discarded back out on the street with nothing.

Ernst began to feel ill. He'd never thought of his work as something that would lead to this kind of treatment of innocent people. After this realization, his work began to slip. Even if he did find evidence that linked someone to a spy group, he didn't turn it in. He often buried it in the mountains of paper work that filled his office. His heart was just no longer in it.

In 1944, Germany was no longer "winning" the war and Ernst knew it. Even though all of the propaganda said they were, Ernst knew it was a lie. Finally, the day came that an order was issued that everyone in his group be given a gun. They were to be assigned to an army unit at the battle front.

That winter was brutal. They lost battle after battle to the Americans. Ernst didn't know how much longer he could bear the cold, the battles, the hunger, and the running and hiding.

Then spring came and the German armies surrendered. Ernst was left to fend for himself deep in Germany. He just wanted to go home. Over the next weeks, he walked and caught rides back to Warsaw. When he got there he was shocked. There wasn't a building left standing. One of the most beautiful cities in Europe was totally destroyed.

He made his way to where his home had been. There was nothing left except piles and piles of bombed out buildings. As he stood looking over the rubble, he saw an old woman crawl out of a hole in the rubble.

"Ernst!" she called out. "Over here! Where did you come from?"

Ernst looked around and saw a withered, ragged old woman he didn't recognize. He stared at her and then his mouth gaped open as he realized who she was. She had been their neighbor across the street from his childhood home. She was a beautiful classy lady back then. When she was twenty five and he was twelve, he told himself he would like to find someone like her when he got older. Now, she looked like she had aged fifty years since the last time he'd seen her four years ago.

She came over to him and hugged him. "It's so good to see you." Then she looked around. "We can't be out here like this. Come with me."

She led him to the 'hole' she had just climbed out of. Then she sat down and wiggled back into it. Once she was inside, she motioned for him to follow. He sat down and slid through the opening.

When his eyes adjusted, he saw that he was sitting on the top of a set of stairs that led down to a large open room full of beds and people. She took him by his hand and introduced him to many of the people there as she pulled him along to a corner of the room. He realized this was where she lived.

"You can't stay here," she told him. "There are Russians everywhere and if they see you, especially in that uniform they'll take you away. They say that they need to 'question' people for security but then people just disappear. We had one man escape and get back here without being caught again. He said there was no questioning. The men were just sent to Russian work camps or shot. The Russians hate the Germans - especially those who served in the army."

"But I need to find my mother and sister."

"They left over a year and a half ago. They were going back to your grandfather's farm in Germany. Do you know where that is? I got a letter from your mother about four months after she left saying that they had made it there and if I saw you or your father to tell you where they were. I will give you some food. Then we'll wait until dark. You must get out of Warsaw and never come back. Now sit down and try to sleep for a while—you'll need it."

Ernst woke to the sounds of people talking and running. He felt a hand grab his and pull him up. His elderly neighbor dragged him through a maze of large and small rooms and up some stairs. At the top, they emerged into the cool night air.

It was then he realized he had left his military jacket behind. She pushed a half loaf of bread at him and said, "Here, this is all the food I have right now. Go, get out of Warsaw. Tell your mother I said hi when you see her." She turned and disappeared back into the crumbled building.

Ernst walked south day after long day, back into Germany. The bread was gone, he was tired, hungry, and without his jacket, he was always cold. One evening, just at sunset, he stopped and looked down at a half blown out building that was full of people. There were lights, talking, music, laughter and the smell of food. Who were these people?

There were lots of lights. They weren't quiet or trying to hide. There was talking and laughing. Oh how long it had been since he had heard people laughing—and the smell of food! Hunger had become a common thing in his life over the past year.

He saw an old metal stove positioned right up against the rock wall, halfway out of the blown out side of the building. The stove glowed with the light of a fire. It had big pots sitting on the top, with people standing around it.

As tired, cold and hungry as he was, he was still leery of moving down into a crowd of people he didn't know. That had been a dangerous thing to do this past year. It was then he heard someone coming up behind him, whistling. The man approached him and seemed friendly enough. He greeted him and introduced himself. At that point, Ernst overcame his fear of unknown crowds and accepted an invitation to join the gathering. It was great to be included in a group of people obviously enjoying themselves and so friendly.

After spending that night and the next morning with these kind people, he was again on his way to his grandfather's farm. It was just a week or so walk and he'd hoped for maybe getting a ride. If he did, he could be there in just a few days.

That evening, as Ernst was beginning to think about where he was going to sleep, he noticed a lady down the road pulling a large dead tree branch behind her. She was having quite a time with it. Ernst walked up and asked if he could help her. She spun around in surprise.

"Sorry," he reassured her. "I didn't mean to scare you. Just thought you looked like you could use some help."

She looked at him, sized him up and finally said, "Yes that would be fine. I just live over there." She pointed to a small house a little way down the road. "I needed more firewood to keep my children warm and to cook with."

Ernst dragged the branch along the road, following the woman. When they got to the house she told him to put it around back. After he dragged the wood to the back of the house he saw the woman and two young children watching him.

"Can I cut it up for you?" he asked. "Do you have a saw or an axe?"

She nodded, disappeared then returned with a small saw and a hatchet.

"You are welcome to come in and have

some bread and milk if you'd like." Then she turned, gathered her children and walked into the house.

Ernst snapped off the smaller limbs still hanging on and broke them into kindling and took them into the house. He was introduced to the two children and offered a small piece of bread. He took the bread and looked through an open door of a small room where there was a bed in which lay a third child.

The woman noticed his glance. "He's four. He has had a high temp for the last three days and I can't get it to come down. I wish I had something more than bread and milk to feed him. Some soup maybe."

Ernst reached into his pocket and pulled out the drumsticks wrapped in paper and handed them to the mother. "Will these make good soup?"

She looked surprised, then grateful. "Yes, they will make a good broth. I don't have anything else to put with it but a few herbs I dried last fall. I'll do the best I can with these."

Ernst again reached into his coat pocket

and pulled out three carrots, an onion and four potatoes. "Will these help?"

The mother just stared at what he had in his hands. Then tears filled her eyes. "Where did you get so many vegetables? I haven't had any since last fall."

Ernst smiled, "They kind of came with the coat. I'll go cut up some more wood while you make some soup."

He worked on the wood for about an hour or so. It was a struggle because the saw and hatchet were very dull. But he did get about half the branch cut up before it got too dark to see. He gathered up what he had and took it into the house.

It smelled wonderful inside—the smell of fresh baked bread and hot soup. He didn't know what herbs she put in the soup but it sure smelled good.

Ernst stacked the wood in the corner and sat and watched the mother spoon broth into her little son's mouth. The child seemed to be enjoying it. He even seemed to be chewing up some of the vegetables.

When the little boy had fallen asleep in her arms she dished up bowls of soup for her other children, one for Ernst and one for her.

She gave each a small piece of bread and poured a glass of milk for her two children. When she started to pour one for Ernst, he waved his hand. "Save it for the kids."

She gave him a look of gratitude. "You can sleep in front of the fire if you want to. We only have one bed and one blanket. Sorry I can't give you more."

After they'd eaten, she sent her children to bed, cleaned up the kitchen and went into the bedroom and closed the door.

Ernst lay down on the floor in front of the fireplace grateful to be warm, dry and well-fed. Just then the door to the bedroom opened and the oldest child came out and handed him a pillow, smiled and returned to the bedroom.

"Well, that's nice," Ernst thought to himself. "A pillow is more than I've had in a long time." He laid his head on the pillow, curled up and dozed off. He woke up once to find the fire was down to just coals. He put a few more pieces of wood on it and watched it come back to life again. Then put his head on the pillow and closed his eyes again.

Suddenly he realized someone was standing in front of him. He jerked awake.

There stood the youngest boy, with tousled, sandy brown hair, rumpled night shirt, bare feet and large blue eyes staring at him.

"What are you doing out of bed?" Ernst asked.

The boy just looked at him. Ernst reached out and felt his face. The child was still a little warm. "You need to go back to bed."

The boy's eyes narrowed then he finally asked, "Are you God?"

The question took Ernst back. "No I'm not God."

"Well Mama said you came from heaven so you must be God."

Ernst smiled. "I'm no God, just a guy trying to get home. You need to go back to bed. You're still sick."

"I can't. I got bumped out of bed. There's no room."

Ernst unbuttoned his coat and motioned for the boy to lie down next to him. The boy snuggled under the coat, then he looked up at Ernst and asked, "Is heaven pretty where you live?"

Ernst again felt the corners of his mouth

turn up. "Yes, heaven is pretty everywhere. Now go to sleep."

Ernst watched the child snuggle under the coat. Within minutes the boy was asleep. Ernst watched the fire for a while and he laughed. "Me, God! That's funny." He made sure the child next to him was covered, then rested his head back onto the pillow and drifted off into a deep and restful sleep.

The next morning, Ernst was awakened by the sounds of children playing. Opening his eyes he saw three children laughing and playing on the floor not far from him. He glanced over at their mother.

"Yes, he's feeling much better this morning. Thank you for all your help. I've wrapped up some bread for you to take with you. You said it wasn't very far from here so I hope this will be enough to see you to your home. Thanks again for everything."

"I don't want to take your food. I have enough to make it home." As he reached into his pocket he felt one of the apples. He smiled, asked for a knife, sat down at the table and cut up the apple into small pieces. One by one the children came to the table and watched him. He began handing out the apple, a piece at a time, to the children. They loved every bite. When he offered one to their mother she shook her head no.

"You need it as much as they do," he insisted. "If you get sick, who will take care of them?"

She took it and savored it as she ate it.

All three children gave Ernst a hug before he left and said their thanks too. The youngest one hugged him the longest and then said, "Thanks for the food and for letting me sleep with you God. Bye." It gave Ernst a lump in his throat. He smiled and waved good-bye.

∾

ERNST MET MORE people along the way who all treated him with kindness and respect. One lady asked him if he was a government official. A few people stopped him and asked questions like was Hitler really dead and were the Americans going to kill them or put them in work camps like the Russians.

"It must be the coat," Ernst thought. It wasn't worn out like most people's coats these days and it was very stylish looking. So maybe they thought he was someone important. Right now, on this cold day, he was glad he was just nice and warm and getting closer to home with every step.

The weather was cold but sunny. Ernst was enjoying the morning sunshine as he walked, thinking about his mother and sister and the young family he'd met two days ago. As he looked down the road he saw a young man coming his way. He wasn't worried because in the past few days, everyone he had met had been very positive and helpful.

Then he stopped short. The young man walking towards him suddenly pulled a gun from his belt. He waved it in Ernst's direction.

Ernst put his hands in the air. "Hey son,

the war's over. Is there something I can do for you so you'll put that gun away?" He could see that this "man" was just a boy.

"Where are you going?" asked the boy.

"To my Grandfather's farm. It's less than a day's walk from here. It's just on the other side of the hill there." He moved his head towards the tree and bush covered hill next to the road.

"Take off the coat and leave it on the road and go." The boy demanded.

Ernst liked the coat but it wasn't worth dying over. He did what he was told. He slipped off the coat, let it fall to the ground and walked up the hill into the trees. His spine tingled, anticipating a bullet at any moment.

As soon as he could, he ducked behind a large bush and carefully peeked down at the boy.

The boy picked up the coat and then sat down along the edge of the road. He stared at his gun for several minutes, then abruptly tossed it into the bushes. Then he buried his face in the coat and appeared to be crying.

Suddenly his head came up, he stood up, put the coat on and started walking.

"I hope he makes it to where he's going," thought Ernst. "I pray the coat will give him renewed hope as it did me and help him as much as it has me."

Ernst walked for the rest of the day, staying off the road, weaving in and out among the trees. He walked until he came to a clearing where he stopped and looked down on his Grandfather's farm.

His eyes filled with tears. There was his mother!

She was taking the clean clothes off the clothes line, just like he remembered her doing so many times when he was growing up.

He was home!

CHAPTER 5

VIKTOR

VIKTOR GREW UP IN AUSTRIA, just outside of Salzburg. He was the youngest of four children and his mother catered to him. He was good in school but loved playing all kinds of sports.

At the age of twelve he became part of a Hitler Youth Group camp in the Bavarian Alps near the border of Austria. Viktor, being almost nine years younger than his next oldest sibling, was thrilled to have hundreds of boys his age to play and do things with. He loved all of the activities at the camp. They hiked, swam, exercised, and played soccer. They had a shooting range and an archery range. Those were his favorites. He became very proficient with a gun and could put his arrows in the bullseye of the target nine times out of ten.

The camp had political rallies at least once a week. They were held in a large stadium filled with Nazi flags and huge banners, proudly displaying the youth motto: "Blood and Honor."

They sang, marched and listened to special speakers who came from all over the country. The speakers gave talks about how wonderful the "Fatherland" was. They talked about how Germany was winning the war and would soon rule the world.

After each speech was over, they stood and saluted the flag and recited the Hitler Youth oath: "I hereby vow and swear with a solemn oath, that I will always do my duty in the Hitler Youth. I do this out of love and loyalty to the Führer and our flag."

Viktor loved all of the physical things they did. But he was finding himself somewhat cold and unfeeling about all of the Nazi philosophy. The more he heard, the more questions he had. But in the end, he pushed the doubt aside and just enjoyed all the other things he loved doing.

He had been hired to help with maintaining the camp, so he stayed for both the summer and the winter. The mountains were beautiful and far away from the destruction of war. Viktor never listened to the older people who talked about negative things of the war. He had been taught not to listen to people that talked that way.

He hadn't been home in over two years, so in February 1945 when word came that all "young men" of the Hitler Youth, 13 and older, would be required to join the army and help with the "final push to victory," Viktor was excited. He was in excellent physical shape and felt that he could be a great help to the Fatherland's fight for victory. He was eager to help.

The boys were loaded into trucks heading away from the beloved mountains. Viktor was surprised that they were not issued a uniform. They were not given combat boots. They were not given helmets or guns. They were told when they got to where they were going they'd find everything they needed.

The farther they got away from the Alps the more devastated the country looked. Towns they drove through were reduced to mostly rubble. The people were gaunt and raggedly dressed as they ran alongside the trucks. Viktor was dismayed at their condition as they begged the occupants of the trucks for food.

When they reached the train station, they were unloaded from the trucks and told to wait for the next train. The small boxed lunch they were given back at Youth Camp was gone so he threw the box away. Viktor was getting hungry and thirsty.

He noticed a water faucet at one end of the station with a long line of people behind it. People were filling up bottles with water. After watching for a few minutes he turned and went back to the trash and retrieved a bottle from the box that his lunch had been in. He then went back to the line and waited for his turn to get water. When he got to the front, he filled the bottle half full and shook it.

He was going to pour it out, but the women behind him said, "Don't pour it out. It still has some juice in it and you'll need every bit of nutrition you can get."

So Viktor drank it down, filled his bottle again and drank that one too. He filled it a third time. He was just about to drink that one when someone in line yelled, "Get out of line, you've had your turn!" So he moved over and joined the rest of his group to wait for the train.

When the train came, he was one of the first ones on. He got a window seat. The train was cluttered, dirty and smelled of trash, sweat, dried blood and hopelessness.

He opened his window and looked at the country passing by. He saw destruction in every direction. Homes burnt out, towns blown apart, dead animals along the tracks and roads and people standing around fires trying to cook something to eat. This was not what they had been told in Youth Camp.

At one station the train stopped and two old women got on. They had baskets full of bread. They were followed by a soldier, gun in hand, watching them. The two old women pasted out slices of bread to everyone.

When one of the ladies got to Viktor she gave him two slices of bread. He smiled and said thank you. Her face showed no emotion. She looked quickly over her shoulder at the soldier and saw he was talking to someone. So she scooped up the last slice of bread and tucked it into her blouse. She looked back at Viktor and he could see a hint of fear in her face. When Viktor said nothing she just walked to the end of the train and got off. She was followed by the other old woman and the guard.

Nothing he saw was like what they'd been told at the Youth Camp. For a country that was 'winning the war' and would 'rule the world,' it sure looked like a mess.

As the train started moving again, an army officer suddenly stood up in front. He said, "There has been a change of fortune in the fighting at the front. Our forces have been forced to retreat. Many have been killed or taken prisoner. Almost all of our forward positions have been overrun or surrounded. Orders have come down from High Command for this group to report to the Russian front to reinforce our forces there." Viktor was surprised and then excited at the news. He would soon get to fight for the Fatherland!

The whole group of Hitler Youth Camp boys traveled in trains and trucks for about two weeks. Much of the time was spent waiting for other trains or trucks to pass.

Often there were breakdowns and they had to wait for things to be fixed. Today, they were told they were only fifty miles from the battlefront and they were to walk the rest of the way there. They walked all that day. They hid in the bushes or trenches when planes would fly over and shoot at them.

Viktor had never seen a dead body before coming here. Two weeks ago he encountered his first one and it shocked him.

Now, many of the boys were picking up guns, helmets, boots, coats and personal things off the dead. Viktor was cold, but the thought of stripping a coat off of a dead man and wearing it, revolted him. He decided he'd rather be cold.

Two days later, they heard a car coming down the road. Everyone hid until they saw it was a German car. They climbed out of their hiding places and flagged it down. "What are all of you doing here?" asked the officer in the car.

"We're headed for the front. Is it close?"

"The war is over," the officer said coldly. "Germany surrendered six days ago."

"We hadn't heard. What are we supposed to do now?" asked Viktor.

The officer didn't look at him, but just gazed out into the field.

"Go home," was all he said. Then he waved his arm at the man driving the car and they drove off down the road leaving about fifty boys standing around not knowing what to do.

Some said that they were going to go to the front lines and fight even if Germany had surrendered. Others seemed undecided about what to do. But Viktor did an almost immediate about face and started walking in the direction of home. Today was his sixteenth birthday.

After a day or two of walking, he knew he needed help. So when he came to a small town he wandered in the streets looking for food and water. It was getting dark and he didn't know where to go or what to do. Just then a young man about his age tapped him on the shoulder. "What are you doing here?" There's a curfew on and you need to get off the street or you may be shot. Where are you going?"

"I have no place to go. I'm just looking for something to eat and some water." Viktor answered.

The boy looked around anxiously. "Come with me. I'll take you home." The two young men dipped in and out of back passageways and dark streets until they came out at a small home on the edge of the town.

When he opened the door to the house Viktor saw an older couple sitting at a kitchen table eating soup. They looked up in surprise. Then the old women got up and poured the last of the soup out of a large pot into a bowl. She put a spoon in it, picked up a slice of bread, and waved at the table showing where Viktor could sit to eat.

While Viktor ate, he listened to the old man and boy talking. They were speaking in Polish, but as they talked, Viktor noticed them pointing to the door and pointing at him. Viktor assumed the old man was asking where the boy had found him. As the old man sat back in his chair, Viktor assumed the boy had told him that he was wandering the street with no place to go.

As Viktor continued to eat, the old man sat thinking for a few minutes. He then sat up and said, "Okay. We need to help those that are hungry. He can sleep in the barn with the rest you have found and brought here tonight."

Viktor listened to them talking but could only understand some of their Polish words. He really didn't care. He was busy eating his soup and drinking the water that was brought to him.

After Victor finished his third glass of water and all of his soup, he picked up his slice of bread and slowly began to eat it. It had a small amount of butter on it and it tasted wonderful. He turned to the women and said "thank you" in German.

The woman who fed him just stared at Viktor for a few seconds. Then turned to the old man and said, "He's German! Are you sure we should let him stay here?"

The old man looked at her with tenderness in his eyes. "The war is over. None of us are blameless. We've all done things to survive these last few years that we may not be too proud of. Besides he's just a boy, not much older than our boy. We'll let him sleep here tonight and send him on his way in the morning." He turned to his boy and said, "Show him where he can sleep please."

The boy motioned for Viktor to follow

him and Viktor did. They exited the house by way of a side door that opened up into a stable. In better days, the cows, horses and chickens would be kept there. But now, the floor had four men lying on it. They were curled up in the straw, trying to sleep.

Viktor found a corner with a large pile of straw and sat down. He snuggled into it and moved the straw around to make himself a bed. He found it was very comfortable compared to where he had been sleeping. He would soon be asleep.

Just before he nodded off, he looked at the strange clothes the other men in the room were wearing. He wondered why they were all dressed alike and why they wore clothing with vertical black and white stripes. The only other time he had witnessed clothing like that was when he saw prisoners working beside the roadway. He decided he'd ask them about their peculiar style of dress in the morning.

When Viktor woke up in the morning, he was surprised to find everyone was gone. No older couple, no boy and no men. He wondered if he was safe there now. It made him nervous that no one had woke him and told him what was going on. He decided his best course of action was to get out of there now and continue walking toward home.

Viktor made it to the border of Germany that day. He was happy to be out of Poland. In Poland, there was so much destruction, so much sorrow, so much death. He was sure that Germany would be better.

But he soon found he was wrong.

As he walked, all he saw in every direction, were crumbled down buildings and starving people. People were living in whatever shelter they could find in this devastated country. There was very little food. People wandering around lost in their own struggles, just trying to survive the day.

As Viktor walked on down the road, he saw a stump and stopped to sit down. He was tired, hungry, thirsty and discouraged. He had come to the conclusion that everything he'd been told the last few years was a lie. Germany wasn't the great country that they had been told it was. They did not win the war nor would they rule the world.

As he looked around, he saw a Lugar lying on the ground. He walked over and picked it up. "This may come in handy," he thought. In checking it over, he found the clip was empty. The lack of ammunition initially concerned him. But as he thought it over, he decided that no one else would know he had no ammunition in that pistol. So he put it in his belt.

As he walked on through the dark, gray day, the road seemed long and unforgiving. It was starting to get cold and Viktor was shivering.

Unexpectedly he saw a man coming toward him in a long black coat.

Viktor worried about what this man may do. He had seen people being hassled by others for food, clothes, or a place to sleep for the night. It had made him a bit paranoid and he reached for the gun.

Then he smiled to himself a little. What did he have that anyone would want? He had no money, food, water or clothes worth anything. All he had on him was the knife that he was given when he first went to Hitler Youth Camp and a gun with no bullets.

But before he could put the gun away he heard, "Hey son, the war is over. Is there something I can do for you so you'll put that gun away?" Looking up, he saw a man with his hands up and a smile on his face.

"Where are you going?" Viktor asked sharply, as if he cared. He just wanted to sound like he had some authority. That was always what they asked at checkpoints.

"I'm going to my Grandfather's farm that is just a short distance over the hill there." The man pointed to the small rise next to the road. "My mother and sister are there and I haven't seen them in three years."

Viktor was shivering again, some from the cold and some from just being scared.

"I want your coat," he said and waved the gun.

"Okay, no problem." The man unbuttoned his coat and started to take it off. Viktor watched him closely making sure that he had no weapons. Not that he could do much if he did.

"Just leave it there on the ground and go," Viktor said, waving his gun in the direction of the hill.

He watched the man climb the hill and disappear into the trees. Then he went over and picked up the coat and sat down alongside the road. His knees were a little wobbly from the confrontation.

"What am I doing?" he thought. "That man was a German just like me! And just like me, he was doubtless lied to as well. Just like me, I'm sure he just wanted to go home and find his family." He looked at the gun in his hand for a long moment, and then gave it a throw into the bushes. He picked up the coat, put it against his face, and sobbed.

The crying didn't last long, just a few minutes. Words came to his mind that said: "Viktor – Stand up and move forward, there is still life to live. You are not alone."

Viktor stood up, wiped the tears from his

eyes and put on the coat. Then once again he began walking to the south and home.

As he walked, the cold wind cut into him. So he buttoned up the coat and stuck his hands into the pockets. To his surprise, he pulled out an apple from one pocket and four potatoes and an onion from the other. He couldn't believe it. He found a tree near the side of the road and sat down. He leaned against the tree and ate his apple. All of the apple, skin, stem, seeds - everything. It was great!

Prior to his last encounter, he had begun to wonder if he would ever make it home. But now that he was warm and had something to eat, he thought he just might make it after all.

After long cold, hungry days of walking, he finally crossed the border into Austria. Viktor was weak, sick and starving. The potatoes and onion were eaten days ago and he felt so tired he could hardly move. He thought: "At last I'm in Austria."

Exhausted, he sat down to rest on the bank of the road. He closed his eyes and thought: "If I could just sleep for a few minutes, I'm sure I would feel better." Hearing birds above him he looked up and watched them fly by. How wonderful it would be to just fly off to somewhere else that wasn't cold and where there was food. He closed his eyes and began to dream of flying as he drifted off to sleep.

Viktor woke with a start. When he opened his eyes he saw an American jeep with two soldiers stopping right in front of him.

Viktor sat up with a jerk. Seeing that they were Americans his adrenalin started flowing. What were they going to do to him?

THE OFFICER STEPPED out of the jeep and walked to where Viktor was sitting and asked, in perfect German, "Where are you headed son and what is that insignia on your sleeve?"

Viktor was shocked. First, because the man spoke flawless German, and second because the man was smiling, and third because he hadn't ever noticed that he had anything on the sleeve of the coat. Inspecting his sleeve, he found that the insignia referred to were brown stitches neatly sewed into the sleeve.

"I'm going to Salzburg. It's my home. I don't know what the insignia on my sleeve is. Someone gave me this coat." A bit of a stretch of the truth.

"Well," the captain said, "if you want a ride, we can take you as far as the turn off to Vienna. Just hop in the back."

Viktor climbed in the back of the jeep as the captain climbed into his seat. The driver revved the engine and the Jeep moved off down the road.

"This is so much easier than walking," Viktor thought, as he laid his head back and relaxed. He listened to the two Americans, but he didn't understand what they were saying.

As he closed his eyes, he made himself a promise: "If I ever get to go to school again, I'm going to learn English."

As Viktor sat in the back seat of the Jeep feeling lucky to have found a ride, the captain spoke to his companion, "Sergeant where are those sandwiches you made this morning before we left?"

"You're not thinking of giving them to

that kid are you? I'll starve before we get back to Vienna."

"I think the kid in the back *is* starving. You'll make it okay but I'm not sure he will without some food. Now where are they?"

"They're in the knapsack sir," the sergeant answered with a groan. The captain reached into the knapsack and pulled out one of the sandwiches. He handed it to Viktor and told him to eat.

Viktor slowly unwrapped the wax paper from the sandwich and just stared at it. It was the most beautiful sandwich he had ever seen. It had scrambled eggs, bacon, slices of onion, tomato and a mound of lettuce. It was all held together by a top and bottom bun with sesame seeds on top. When he finally tasted it, he determined it was beyond anything he could remember eating. He savored every little bite. It was unbelievably magnificent.

A little further down the road, the captain handed him a canteen of water. Viktor was so thirsty that he drank it all. With a full stomach and his thirst quenched, he relaxed, closed his eyes and was soon asleep.

He was awakened by the captain pulling

on his leg. "Hey kid. This is your stop. Vienna is this way and Salzburg is that way." Viktor climbed out of the Jeep, thanked the captain, and began to walk away. But after a couple of steps, he stopped and turned back.

"Can I ask you a question?" Viktor asked.

"Sure" the captain said.

Viktor reached into his pocket and pulled out the can he had carried with him for the last few days.

"What is this?" The captain looked at what Viktor was holding and at first grinned from ear to ear. Soon he was not only grinning, but was bent over in laughter.

"Who gave you a can of Spam?" he asked.

When the laughter stopped, he explained to Viktor what it was and how to use the key on the top to open the can. Then, he turned back to the jeep, reached in the knapsack and pulled out another sandwich and handed it to Viktor.

"Eat this first and save that Spam for another day." The captain said goodbye, climbed into the jeep and rode away leaving Viktor in their dust.

Viktor watched them go, then wondered to himself how to thank someone he'd never met before and would never meet again. "They saved my life. If there is a God I suppose I should thank Him." Then Viktor started to walk in the direction of home.

SALZBURG HAD BEEN BOMBED in the war but only about half of the city had been destroyed. Viktor was relieved to see that much of the city was still standing and beautiful.

As he turned down the street of his childhood home, he was excited to see that the street looked much the same as he remembered it. As he got to his old house, he was about to open the door when he suddenly wondered: "I wonder if my family still lives here?"

He decided, rather than just opening the door and walking in, it would be better to knock and let whoever was inside open it.

He knocked once, no answer. He knocked again. When the door opened, he was gazing into the loving eyes of his mother. He just stood there for a few moments and then simply fell into her arms.

He was finally home.

For the next two weeks, Viktor did nothing but sleep and eat. One afternoon he came into the living room to see his mother sewing a little girl's dress.

"Who's that for?" he asked.

"It's for the little girl next door," his mother said. "She starts school tomorrow and all of her dresses are too small for her. She lost her Dad and all her siblings in the war, so she and her mother came to live with her grandmother next door. She is a lovely little girl.

"As I got to know her, I found myself feeling like I needed to do something to help her be accepted at school. I rummaged around and found some material I had hidden away during the war. I decided I would use it to make her a dress for school. The problem is I have no buttons to put on it. There isn't a store in town that has any. I guess I'll have to cut some off my dress."

Viktor thought about it for a minute then said, "Give me your scissors." He took the scissors and went into the front hall. He found his coat and cut the decorative buttons off both sleeves. He then brought the buttons back to his mother and asked, "They're black. But will they do?" He handed her six small black buttons.

She looked at them and smiled. "Yes, where did you get these?"

"From the coat I was wearing when I first got home."

"Where did you find that coat? It is a very nice coat."

Viktor thought about the question for a minute and then said, "It was gift to me when I really needed it." Again, his answer was a stretch of reality.

"Well," his mother said, "they will work just fine. And by the way, you will be going to school tomorrow too."

The next day the little girl stopped in to thank Viktor's mother for the dress. "Everyone at school thought it was the most beautiful dress they've seen in a long time. It was the best day I've had forever. I have lots of friends, a new dress, and I get to go to school again. I'm so happy today. Thank you very much."

Viktor did go back to school the next day and almost every day thereafter for the next seven years. He finished Primary school, went on to get his bachelor's degree, a master's, and then a Ph.D. He loved science and research projects. But what he was good at was teaching the history of the Third Reich. So that was what he finally did. He began teaching classes in history at the University of Salzburg and each semester his classes grew larger and larger. He became one of the most popular professors on campus.

When the weather was cold, he would wear his beloved coat.

As he began a new semester, he was telling a new class what they would be covering in the class when he noticed a beautiful young lady in the fourth row that repeatedly drew his attention.

As the weeks passed many of the students would stay after class to ask more questions and talk. One of them was the girl Viktor had noticed on the first day of class. He found out that her name was Karlie and was surprised to find out that she was from America. "But your German is so good. No accent at all."

"I've been told that before," she answered. "My parents were from Germany and moved to the U.S. before the war. My brother and I were young so we picked up

English fast but at home we still spoke German. When the war began I was a young teenager. My mother and father were worried about their poor English. They didn't want to sound so German and wanted to learn to talk better. So every evening after I finished my homework I would spend an hour or two teaching English to my parents."

"When the war ended I listen to my brother talk about how great and resilient the German and Austrian people were. He was stationed in Austria after the war to help with the reconstruction. So when I finished my bachelor's degree I decided I'd like to come here and study the history of Germany and Austria.

Viktor listened to her story, impressed. Then he said, "So then you know how to teach English to an Austrian. How would you like to teach me English? I've always wanted to learn."

"I'd love to do that," Karlie said.

It was just a couple of hours a week in the beginning. Then it became most evenings. Then there were lunches that morphed into long evening dinners by candlelight. It wasn't long before Viktor was totally infatuated with Karlie.

He was watching her from a distance one day as she was working on a class project with other classmates. As he watched her, he realized he wanted her—no needed her in his life. He felt the desire to protect her and to keep her safe and happy. Two days later, he asked her to marry him. With a broad smile and a big hug, she said yes.

The next two years were full and happy for them. He continued to teach and Karlie took classes. In their spare time Viktor took Karlie site-seeing all over Austria and much of Germany.

When she finished her degree, she told him she wanted to go back home to America. He agreed to take her, and immediately applied for a professorship at several universities. Eventually, he was accepted at the University of Utah. One month after being told he had been accepted, he received an acceptance letter from the university.

Viktor was nervous about traveling to a place he had never been before. But Karlie was ecstatic to be going back home. She missed it so.

After formulating a plan to move, Viktor obtained passage on a steam ship to New York City and train tickets from New York to Salt Lake City.

When the day of their move finally arrived, they traveled to the coast and boarded the ship bound for America. As the ship moved out to sea, Viktor watched Europe recede in the distance. He wondered if he would ever see it again.

It was a stormy voyage, but they endured it well and arrived in good spirits, healthy and happy.

The ride across the continent on the train was overwhelming for Viktor. He was amazed at the variety and vastness of the landscape they were passing through. After many miles had passed by their window Viktor felt lost in this foreign land, but Karlie was aglow with the realization that she was going home at last.

Once there, they began a search for a place to live. After a week or so, they found and settled into a small apartment on the hill near the university.

She was so excited to do what Viktor had done for her in Austria. She began to introduce him to many of the places of interest in and around Utah. They visited Saltair, the amusement park built out into the Salt Lake. They traveled to state parks like Bryce, Mesa Verde and Zion. Karlie convinced Victor to take her to Disneyland in California and Carlsbad Caverns in New Mexico. Top on her list was a visit to Yellowstone National Park where Victor experienced hot pools, geysers and mud pots; things not seen in Europe. He was amazed at the sight of large herds of elk and buffalo. He was taken back when black bears and grizzly bears came right up to the car begging for treats.

Shortly after the visit to Yellowstone, Karlie asked Viktor for a night out as a change in routine. He agreed that sounded like fun. Over dinner, Karlie announced she had a surprise for him. She told him he was going to become a poppa! Viktor was surprised at first. This was new territory for them. But as the idea of becoming a father sunk in, he was overjoyed. Six months later, Viktor and Karlie became new parents of a bouncing baby boy. He was small, pink and perfect.

Eighteen months later, they welcomed a

second son into their lives – also a healthy baby. With the new baby and a toddler under foot, the little apartment they were living in became cramped for their growing family.

After a long search, the couple found just the house for them. It had plenty of space for a kitchen, front room and even a nursery. There was also a large back yard, a garage, white picket fences and lots of shade trees. They were excited to find such a wonderful house with payments that wouldn't break their budget.

Over the next few years, Viktor and Karlie welcomed two little girls into their lives. These cute little darlings fit nicely into their parent's lives and brought joy and laughter into the home – especially for the poppa of the house. Their home was filling up with a happy and loving family.

Just before daughter number two was born, Karlie began to clean out closets and some boxes that had never been opened since the apartment. In cleaning, Karlie ran across Viktor's old black coat. She looked it over and decided it was time for the coat to go. She placed it in a pile destined to be thrown away.

When Viktor arrived home that evening, he found that his wife had been cleaning out the far corners of their home. He asked why the cleaning spurt just now. She said, "We need to get rid of all the old stuff we no longer need. You know we are expecting again and need to make room."

As Viktor looked around, he noticed a black sleeve hanging out of the trash bin. Upon further inspection, he found it was the treasured old black coat given him so many years ago.

He said, "Why are you throwing this away? You know I love and treasure this old thing."

Karlie said, "Come sit on the bed, right here next to me." As Viktor did, Karlie said, "Look at the coat, Honey. The sleeves are frayed, the collar needs to be sewn back down, the lining is hanging out at the elbows – it's a mess! I know you love it and it has served you well. But it is time for it to go. You never wear it anymore and goodness knows, nobody else is going to want it. It is time to throw it away."

Just then the phone rang. As Karlie ran to answer it, Viktor sat and stared at the old black coat in his hands.

"How can I toss it away?" he thought. "It saved my life more than once." He buried his face in the coat, just as he had done many times in his life. As before, it seemed to help him think through his problems and give him comfort.

As he sat like this, the words came to his mind that he heard years before at the age of sixteen, when he first got this coat.

They were the words that had brought rain to the desert of his heart.

"Viktor - Stand up and move forward, there is still life to live. You are not alone."

They were the words that kept him walking toward home all those years ago.

Viktor thought about the recent changes he and Karlie were now facing – they were getting older; before long, the children would become more expensive to support; offers at work to move to a more challenging position were pending; and many others were on the horizon. With all the changes in his life, those same words were exactly what he needed to hear.

Once again, he wiped the tears from his eyes, stood up and walked to the bags and bins in the middle of the room. As he held the coat, he just couldn't bring himself to put it in the trash bin again. Instead, he walked over to the charity bags. He picked out a bag full of clothes, dug halfway down and put the coat in the middle of the bag so Karlie wouldn't see it. He closed the bag and smiled.

"Maybe someone out there will need an old worn-out coat. If there is, I pray it will save them in some way as it saved me." Viktor wiped tears from his eyes as he walked away from the coat.

As Karlie returned, she asked Viktor "What did you decide about the coat?"

"I guess you're right," he said. "I'll take care of it." Feeling a little guilty, he smiled on the inside knowing he had taken care of his old friend – just not the way Karlie expected.

CHAPTER 6

KURT

KURT WAS RAISED by his father. Kurt's mother left him and his dad when Kurt was only six years old. He couldn't remember much about her except the way she smelled. She always smelled like soap and fresh flowery perfume.

His father found a neighbor lady to watch him after school until his father got home from work. Kurt just called her Grandma. She didn't seem to mind. She fed him, helped him with his homework, washed the dirt off of him when he came in from playing, read to him, and when he was sick she rocked him. He was comfortable around her and she often told him that he was a good boy and that she loved having him in her life.

When he was twelve, Grandma died, which again, left a big hole in Kurt's life. Without the love Grandma provided him. Kurt felt lost and alone. He had relied on that love and encouragement Grandma gave him to boost his confidence in himself. At twelve, he wasn't quite ready to become an adult, responsible for making his own way. He confided this to his father. But his father told him he was old enough to take care of himself after school now. So when he got home from school, he had no one to talk to. This gave him lots of time to think.

One night at supper, he asked his father why his mother left.

"Well, she said that she just didn't want to be a wife and mother anymore."

That really bothered Kurt. Had he been such a terrible child, that she didn't want to be a mom? If he had been better, would she have stayed? Did she ever think about him like he did about her?

With his persistent feelings of guilt over his mother leaving him, Kurt soon began to misbehave in school. Of course he was disciplined for his actions which made him even more disillusioned with school.

At the age of sixteen, he told his dad that he wanted to prepare for and take the GED test and be done with school. "I just don't fit with the other kids there. I want to work on helicopters. If I could start that now, that would make me happy." Being very driven and intelligent, Kurt studied hard and took the test. He passed it and soon after applied for tech school.

Because Kurt was only sixteen the local tech school wouldn't take him, so he got a job at an airport as a cleanup person. His job also included lots of other tasks like making sure the planes were tied down, minding the counter, and inventorying parts. He was learning many things from all the people he worked with.

When he turned eighteen and it came time for Kurt to start school, he was sure he was ready. But once he started and really got into the material, he found that it was hard.

"Dad, school is harder than I thought it was going to be."

"I know, Son, some things are difficult

but you've got to keep working through them. You'll make it if you hang in there."

Kurt often went to help his father at his workplace before going on to school. His Dad was a manager of the local Deseret Industries store.

Kurt normally liked helping his dad with whatever needed to be done at the store, but on this particular morning he wasn't looking forward to it.

He had decided his classes were just too hard. He was going to tell his dad that he was quitting school.

When he arrived at the store, his dad was really busy. So instead of burdening him more with his decision to quit school, Kurt decided to wait to tell him.

Instead, he jumped in and helped with sorting the clothes that had come in. Cottons in one bin, polyester in another and things to be made into quilts in a third.

When he came across a worn out old black coat, he asked his Dad what he should do with it.

After looking it over, his dad told him to just throw it away. "It's too worn out to be of any more use."

So that's what Kurt did. He was deep into the sorting task when he felt someone touch his shoulder. He spun around.

"Sorry, I didn't mean to startle you," his father said. "It is time for you to be leaving for school. Don't forget your coat, it's starting to snow. By the way, I will be working late tonight and have an early morning meeting tomorrow. So I won't see you until late tomorrow night. Don't wait up for me."

"Okay Dad. I will see you then." Kurt said to himself "I guess I'll go on to school today. I can wait to tell dad about quitting school tomorrow night."

It was then that he remembered he'd forgotten his coat. Some of his training at school would be outside and without a coat, he would freeze.

Suddenly, he remembered the old black coat in the trash bin. He dug it out, put it on, and headed for school.

The next day when Kurt's father returned home, he and his dad finally sat down to talk. Kurt said, "Dad, I want to quit school. This semester has been just too hard!"

His dad said, "Are you sure? You have put a lot of effort into your schoolwork already. I hate to see you lose that work you have completed."

Kurt said, "I know, but I don't think I am going to make it."

His father said, "Why don't you work really hard till the end of this semester. I am sure you can do it. Then if you want to quit, you will not have lost all the work you have done so far."

After a moment of thought, Kurt decided that if his father was backing him, maybe he could finish this semester. Then he could quit if he wanted to without losing the work he'd done so far.

At the end of the semester, Kurt came home waving his grades in the air and saying "I made it! I passed all of my classes!"

His father said, "See – I knew you could do it. You just need to give yourself a chance, and you can do anything. You know what? I think if you put your mind to it, you could do another semester."

Kurt thought about that for a minute. He said to himself, "I did it this time, maybe I can do it again."

With more passing grades and after frequent long discussions with his father about staying in school, Kurt made it through those late winter snowstorms, into the following summer and into the fall. Kurt discovered school seemed to become easier the longer he was there. He was now confident he would reach his goal of graduating.

The coat kept Kurt warm through spring storms and spent the hot summer riding around the city in the back seat of Kurt's car. When he again began school that fall, on cold days he'd put on the ragged old black coat. It seemed to keep him more immersed in and motivated by what he was doing.

During discussions with one of his professors, the professor commented that Kurt had changed. He said he seemed more focused and grounded lately. He said "By the way, I have often noticed you wearing that old black coat to school. Are you lacking sufficient funds to purchase a new one?"

Kurt responded "No – I picked the old coat up at the Deseret Industries Store one day while helping my dad sort clothes. I had forgotten my coat that day and it was cold out. I intended to just wear it to get me through the day. But after a while, I noticed that I was comfortable wearing it. It somehow made me feel grounded and calm.

"Because it makes me feel that way, I have kept it and have been wearing it often. I have noticed that feeling that way has made me a better student. I am not sure why this has happened, but I too have noticed the change in me and I love it. I am enjoying being on top of the game for a change."

One day, on his way home from school, he called his dad. "I aced the test Dad! It was like someone was just pouring the answers into my head. It was a great feeling."

"That's great Son. Remember what I told you about having good and bad days. *Enjoy the good and remember the bad ones won't last forever.* Got to run, see you tonight."

Kurt rolled his eyes. His Dad was always saying things like that. But one thing he said many times over the years was: *"If you're having a bad day, try not to let it spill onto anyone one else. If you're having a great day, definitely do allow it to spill onto others."*

Kurt just smiled. Since he was doing better, he felt better about himself. He was finding much of what his father had been trying to teach him all these years starting to make sense. "Scary," Kurt thought as he smiled and softly laughed to himself.

What a great day it had been. It had been a beautiful morning with sunshine and warm temps for this time of year. He'd done great on his tests and one of his professors said that two companies were interested in hiring him when he graduated. So even though the day had turned cold and windy, he was still having a good day.

As he drove he heard his dad's words enter his head again, *"Let it spill out onto someone else."* As he sat at a red light he looked to his right and saw an old man sitting on a bench with just a light jacket on. It was getting more windy and cold and Kurt felt sorry for him.

Then, almost without thinking, Kurt drove into the turn lane and almost up on the sidewalk in front of the old man on the bench. Kurt jumped out of his car, reached in the back seat, and picked up his coat. He then walked over to the man and asked him to stand up. The old man did as he was told. Kurt helped him put on the well-worn old black coat.

"I hope this coat will cover you with

warmth and love. It has helped to keep me going through hard times and made me a better person. I know it smells a little like gas. I sometimes have worked in it when I was fixing airplanes. But I'm sure it will keep you warm in this weather."

The old man thanked him. Kurt got back into his car and drove away.

CHAPTER 7

THOMAS GREY

THOMAS GREY WAS BORN and raised in Salt Lake City. He went to school in Logan, Utah and then moved back to Salt Lake. He found a job there with the University of Utah as a maintenance man. Over time, he worked his way up to being the supervisor over maintenance for the entire facility. He remained in that position for many years.

He married his high school sweetheart, had two children and bought a beautiful home. He and his little family enjoyed life together. They frequently took vacations to water parks, and attended ball games and music concerts. They were happy just enjoying each other's company.

Then came the day shortly after his

daughter turned sixteen, that she was diagnosed with a rare form of cancer. She fought the disease valiantly, but lost the battle and died two years later.

Their daughter's death broke Thomas's heart, but his wife took it much harder. She mourned her daughter's loss and did nothing much for almost eighteen months.

Only the college graduation of her son finally lessened her profound feelings of loss. Her son's announcement that he was going to ask his girlfriend to marry him brought more sunshine into her life. She began to live again.

When grandchildren came along, life was full and good again! They were blessed with three grandchildren—two girls and a boy. How they enjoyed them.

Thomas and his wife began to fulfill their roles as grandparents. They took great joy in taking them to the zoo, to the pool, and to ball games. It was just like they had done with their own children. They loved it!

Then, came the late-night call. The man on the other end of the line said Thomas and his wife needed to come to the hospital right now! Their son had been in a car crash and they did not expect him to live. As they arrived at the emergency room, the doctor met them and took them to a private room. He told them the medical team had done everything they could to save their son. But unfortunately, he did not survive.

Following the accident, his daughter-in-law and the grandchildren came often to visit. But as the children began junior high, got involved in school activities and became more involved with friends and other activities, the visits became less frequent.

One day his daughter-in-law came and told him that she and the children were moving back to the Midwest to be close to her parents. Her Dad had a business that he no longer wanted to run. He offered it to her if she wanted it.

"It's a great opportunity," she told Thomas. Within a few short months they were gone.

In the beginning there were lots of phone calls, visits on Thanksgiving, Christmas, spring break and summer vacations. But as the grandchildren grew older, the phone calls became fewer and fewer. Soon it was down to just birthdays and Christmas cards.

His daughter-in-law remarried and moved on to a new life. Contact with their son's family now happened maybe once a year.

Thomas and his wife kept busy with volunteer work and trips. They even took a trip back to the Midwest to see their grandchildren and former daughter-in-law. When they visited, they were tended and cared for in every way. On their visit, they saw lots of interesting things and enjoyed it all. But even though they were treated well, Thomas was happy when the time came to go home. On the plane back to Salt Lake City he had the feeling that he'd never see his grandchildren again. That feeling turned out to be prophetic.

One day, his wife said she was tired and was going to have a nap. Three hours later he checked in on her. Seeing she was still sleeping, he decided to wake her. He called to her and shook her, trying to wake her. He found that he could not. She had died in her sleep. The funeral was small, a few friends and no family.

Thomas was devastated. It was now just him – rattling around in that great big house with all of the memories it brought. It made him lonely. So after a few months of contemplation, Thomas decided to down-size from his beautiful spacious home to a retirement condominium. It would be easier to care for and would provide company in the close neighbors he would have.

Thomas liked talking with the new people in the condo complex, but he was careful not to get too close to anyone. He just didn't want to have the pain of letting go of someone he'd learned to love again.

That's when he decided to start walking the streets of the city.

At first it was just a few blocks. Then it was a mile or two. After doing it for six years, Thomas walked four or five miles or more.

Even at the age of ninety-two, he still loved doing it. He found people he liked to talk to along the way. Some people who lived on the street even knew him by name. Plus, he enjoyed getting outside in all kinds of weather.

People at his complex asked him what he would do if it started to storm or he got too tired to walk home. Thomas would shrug and say, "I'll just call a taxi to take me home."

He thought, "Like that is a hard thing to solve."

Today had started out warm and pleasant, but this afternoon it had turned cold and windy. He sat on a bench, shivering. He was close to walking into the store next to him and calling for a ride home when a car pulled up in front of him.

A young man got out and asked him to stand up. Thomas didn't see any reason to not do what was asked, so he stood up. The young man reached into his car and produced a black woolen coat. He held it up and motioned for Thomas to put it on – so he did.

After he inspected Thomas in the coat, the young man told him he hoped it would keep him warm and apologized for the smell of gas on the coat. Then he smiled and told Thomas the coat was given with love. He then got back into his car, waved goodbye and drove away.

Thomas could feel the tears starting to fill his eyes. He realized again that there were many good people in the world who do simple kind things for people around them.

He said to himself, "We don't hear about them often enough."

The young man was right, the coat did smell a little like gas, but Thomas could already feel himself getting attached to this coat. It was a nice warm coat. Thomas decided to stay a little longer on the bench before he called for a ride.

BRENT HAD BEEN busy all morning long. He leaned back in his chair and stretched. A survey of the paperwork on his desk told him he'd been sitting long enough. He needed to get up and move for a minute.

As he got up, he looked out the small window in his office. There was a man sitting on the bench in front of the bistro. He'd seen the man sitting on that bench before, but he had never thought anything about it.

Today it was cold and windy out and Brent felt sorry for him sitting there in the bad weather. He turned and went out to the kitchen. He asked, "Is there any soup left?"

His son, Leon said, "Yes, about two bowls full. Why?"

"Dish it up. I'll be right back." He put on his coat and walked out the door.

~

BRENT WORKED for the City of Salt Lake for over twenty years and was happy there. But when an old restaurant was put up for sale, he and Elsa started talking about a dream they had had for years. They both always wanted to run a restaurant. But with the pressures of raising the family and their desire to not be gone at night when their children were home, they never got around to doing anything about it.

When the children got older and needed jobs, they reconsidered. They still did not want to be working late at night because of the impact on the family. To get around that problem, they decided to purchase the old restaurant and make the operating hours from seven in the morning to three in the afternoon.

His children all wanted to go to college but none of them wanted to go into debt for it, so they all worked at the family restaurant.

Their twin sons, Leon and Ethan, took

over the kitchen and learned to be excellent chefs.

Marta, their daughter, waited tables, helped with the cleanup and seated guests when needed. She saved enough to pay for her first year of nurse's school. She was in her third semester now and working hard to pay for it.

Leon had finished one semester of college and told his Dad he was going to work full time until January so his next semester would be paid for.

Ethan said he didn't know what he wanted to study yet, so he was just going to work for a year or so.

Brent also wished he was out of debt. The restaurant was doing well, but he still had a mortgage on the building he was in. But all of his children were doing well and Brent and Elsa were proud of them.

Today, Brent was concerned about an old man sitting on a bench in the cold. He wanted to help him.

Brent went outside and asked the old gentleman, "Would you like to come over to my place and have some soup? It's so cold and windy out here, you look like you could use a hot bowl of soup to warm you up. I happen to have one that you could have for free."

The old gentleman refused. But when Brent asked again, he smiled, nodded, and followed Brent back into the bistro.

"My name is Thomas. This is real nice of you. I'd be willing to pay for the soup."

"You don't need to. We'd have to throw it away if you didn't eat it. So you're doing us a favor by eating it."

Thomas smiled. "You own this place? It's really nice."

"Well, yes - me and the bank. Thanks. It is a family run business." Brent called his sons out of the kitchen and introduced them to Thomas. "My wife and daughter work here as well."

"You have a nice family," Thomas said as he looked around.

"Do you have family around here?" Brent asked.

"No I don't. I live in that big new retirement complex up on the hill. I bought a condo there about three years ago and I have friends there but no family."

"Oh sure," Brent said. "I've seen those apartments. They are very nice."

Brent had heard it was an exclusive housing community for retired people with lots of resources at their disposal.

He eyed the man sitting in front of him, eating soup, dressed in a ragged old coat. The guy didn't look like he had two dollars to his name. No way did he live in that posh complex. Great story though.

"Would you like another bowl?" he offered.

"Sure, it's really good soup."

They talked for a while then Thomas said he needed to be getting home. "Can I give you a ride?" Brent asked with a smirk. He knew he would be turned down.

"No thank you. The weather has cleared up some. I think I'll just walk." Brent knew that answer was coming.

"Come by again sometime." Brent said with a smile. He liked talking to the old guy. Thomas nodded as he left, said thanks again and walked out the door. Brent watched him walk up the street wondering where he slept.

Thomas showed up on the bench in front of Brent's bistro about once a week and Brent always went out and invited him in. Thomas slowly got to know the Cox family. They were surprised how much they enjoyed having Thomas around. It got to be a daily get-together except for Thursdays. One day Brent asked Thomas why he never came on Thursday.

"I don't like your 'soup-of-the-day' on Thursday," was his answer.

Brent laughed. "We could feed you something different."

Brent asked Thomas one day if he could get a new coat for him.

"No, I have four or five coats at home but I like wearing this one. It was given to me by someone prompted to help someone he thought was in need. I like that. Besides, for whatever reason, I seem to make more friends when I wear it. People have bought happy meals for me, telling me they hope it would make me happy. Sometimes people just sit down and visit with me. "Truth is I need that. I've been a little lonely since my wife died.

"Sometimes people give me money. I always leave that at whatever church I walk by on my way home. One day I saw a young mother with three little children coming out of a church. She looked tired and worried. So, that day, the money went to her and her children. The amount was $78.91. When I gave it to her, tears sprang up in her eyes and she said "Thank you." I love to do that sort of thing - it's fun."

One day while Thomas was eating, he said he hadn't felt very well the past few days.

Brent looked at him and said, "You look a little pale."

Brent got up and called his wife. "Honey, please call the paramedics."

By the time they arrived, Thomas wanted to lie down. After checking him out, the paramedics took him to the hospital. Brent had Marta check in on him. She said he wasn't doing well at all. Brent and Elsa went up to see him once, but Thomas was just sleeping. He never knew that they were there. Three days later, Thomas Grey died.

Brent had Marta find out which funeral home they sent him to. He looked up the number and called. He knew Thomas didn't have any money. A good man like that should have a proper funeral.

Brent told the man on the other end of the line that he was a friend of Thomas Grey. Then he asked, "Is it possible for me to pay for some of his funeral costs?"

"Oh no, his funeral was paid for ten years ago," said the man on the line. That surprised Brent. At the funeral, Brent was again surprised at how high end everything looked.

Three weeks later, a lawyer showed up at the bistro and asked for Brent. He asked if he could talk for a few minutes.

"You might want to sit down," said the lawyer. "I have a few things for you." When he sat down with the lawyer, he was told that Mr. Thomas Grey had left Brent's family something in his will.

Brent was shocked. As the lawyer read, he became even more blown away.

Mr. Thomas Grey left a scholarship trust fund for all of Brent's children. His children could go to school without the worry of money.

After hearing that, Brent could hardly breathe. The lawyer went on. He handed Brent a piece of paper. As he looked at it, he saw that it was the mortgage document for his restaurant. It said "Paid In Full."

Brent jumped to his feet and stood there – eyes wide! Then the tears started to come as he asked, "So he really had money? He said he did, but by the way he dressed I never believed him."

The lawyer answered, "Yes I know. He and I talked about that more than once. He'd tell me he was in his 90's. He didn't need any new clothes. He had enough to last him until he died. I guess he was right," he said with a smile. "Well, I need to be on my way. If you have any questions, my name is on the paperwork - just call." He shook Brent's hand and left Brent weak-kneed and in tears.

As Brent sat in his office, trying to take it all in, he looked up at the coat rack where they had hung Thomas's old black coat the day he went to the hospital. Brent thought about how they would miss the old gentleman.

Then he looked again at the coat, only harder this time. He sat up in his chair and looked even harder. He finally got up, walked around his desk and took the old black coat off the rack. He ran his fingers down the sleeve of the coat.

It couldn't be! But there they were. Elsa's even stitches she had stitched on the sleeve of his coat a life-time ago. They were dirty and worn, but they were hers.

This was the coat given to him in the streets of Salt Lake City years ago. Brent sat down hard in his chair. How did it get back to him and where had it been all these years? Brent's tears ran down his checks. What a day it had been.

The next morning Brent sat his family down and told them about Thomas and what he had done for the family. There were many tears and much laughter as they talked about Thomas. Finally they had to get ready for breakfast. Leon said he had some errands to run, but would be back in time for the breakfast rush.

"Would you drop this off at the dry cleaners for me?" Brent said, as he handed Leon Thomas' old coat.

"You're going to have this old rag dry cleaned?" Leon looked surprised.

"Please just do it." Brent smiled at his son.

Three days later Brent was standing in front of Pres. George Albert Smith's grave. He walked over and gently laid the coat, still in its dry cleaning bag, over the tomb stone and stepped back.

"Thank you again, sir. This coat saved me not once but twice. I can still feel the power it holds. Thank you. I'm so grateful." He stood there for a long time and then left.

CHAPTER 8

ED AND JOANIE

ED HAD SPENT twenty years in the Army as an airport traffic controller. In those twenty years, he had moved many times and seen a lot of the beautiful places of the world.

Somewhere in those twenty years he met and married Joanie. She was a beautiful, gentle lady who loved children and *him*. They raised three children and outlived four dogs. His oldest boy, Rollin, was 19 and in college. His next one, Hayden, was 17. He just graduated from high school and was trying to decide where he was going to go to college. The youngest son, Tank, just turned 16. As sixteen-year-olds do, he was sure he knew everything. Tank's real name was Charles, but he was always so big, everyone started calling him Tank and the name stuck.

When Ed retired from the army, he told Joanie he wanted a low key, low stress job that would allow him to be outside more than inside. He found it in Salt Lake City.

He started as an assistant manager and was now the manager and head caretaker of the Salt Lake City Cemetery. It kept him busy. There was watering, mowing, fertilizing, weeding, raking leaves, trimming trees and moving the snow off the roads in the cemetery in the winter. In addition, he had to make sure that grave sites were ready for funerals. It was a quiet job where the customers were always happy with what he did for them.

Today he was on cleanup detail. Cleanup day was the day that he and his crew went through the cemetery and cleaned up all the things that people left on the graves to honor their dead loved ones.

Ed was always fascinated at what people left. They included: Plastic flowers, live flowers, pictures, potted plants, flags, pin wheels, letters, books, baby shoes, toys, ballet slippers, ceramic angels, food, stuffed animals and just about everything else you could think of.

But this one today baffled him. As he stood by his pickup and stared, he couldn't figure out why anyone would want to leave a coat draped over President George Albert Smith's tombstone.

An old, well-worn coat at that, and still in a dry cleaning bag. Who would leave an old coat or even take a worn out, ragged old coat like this one to be cleaned! The sleeves of the coat were tattered. The elbows were thread bare around the patches. And the collar was so worn through that the white lining was hanging out and threadbare as well.

Looking at the coat draped over the tombstone made him shake his head. He walked up and picked up the coat. As he did so he heard thunder in the distance. *Rain is coming,* he thought.

As he scanned the sky, out of the corner of his eye he saw her. He'd been looking for her this morning but hadn't seen her yet today. She was a big yellowish-brown dog that had been hanging around the cemetery for the last three or four weeks.

Undoubtedly, someone had dumped a

dog they didn't want. Ed had been putting out some of his lunch for her, but when she'd come to eat, she'd never let him get close. He stopped and watched her for a minute.

"She's looking for her share of my lunch," he thought. However, today she wouldn't get it. On his way to work this morning, he'd stopped and picked up a bag of dog food. He liked eating all his lunch, and he didn't want the dog to go hungry.

He tossed the old coat onto the seat of his pickup through the open window. He then walked around the truck and climbed into the driver's side. He drove a short way up the road to the building where his small office was located. The thunder came again. He rolled up his windows and walked to the door of the building.

He stopped and looked around again for the dog. She was watching him. He smiled and thought "Just wait a few minutes and I'll get you something to eat."

He unlocked the door, went inside, and started looking for something to put the dog food in. He found a small plastic bowl that had been left behind by someone. He washed it out and filled it full of food. He then walked to the door. Just as he got there he heard the rain start to come down in sheets. He reached for the door and opened it just as the thunder rolled across the sky again.

A wet, yellow, flash of fur raced by him, almost knocking him over. She ran for his desk and climbed under it as far as she could get. The lighting outside streaked across the sky and was followed by another loud crack of thunder. The dog, shaking and shivering, wiggled farther under the desk.

"Well," Ed said. "Nice to meet you. I have something for you to eat." He walked over to his desk and looked down at the shaking dog. She was all wet.

"I have something for that too," he said as he sat the bowl of dog food on his desk and ran outside to his truck.

He picked up the coat from the front seat, and tossed the plastic bag it had been in, into the back of his truck with the rest of the trash he'd gathered that day. Then he turned and hurried back inside.

"Here, this should help to dry you off and keep you warm."

He gently laid the coat over the dog and watched as she wiggled herself under it. She burrowed further under the desk as another streak of lighting lit up the sky and the thunder followed close behind.

The storm lasted about a half hour, after which the sun came out and lit up all of the rain drops still clinging to the leaves.

Ed had been sitting in his chair rocking. He made a few phone calls and tried to do some paper work. But it was hard to get anything done with a big dog under his desk.

He watched the storm and wondered where the dog came from and if she belonged to anyone. She finally looked out from under the coat. Ed set a full bowl of food down in front of her.

"Lunch," he said. She slowly got up, smelled the food and started eating. The phone rang. As Ed answered it, he slowly slid the bowl to one side and glided up to his desk.

It was a funeral home, making arrangements for an upcoming internment. He scribbled all the information down and then stood up, walked to the window as if to visualize where the grave would be. He stared out the window for a few more seconds before he realized the crunching of dog food had stopped.

He turned around to see the bowl empty and the dog in the corner with the coat. She was arranging it for her bed. He watched her as she moved the coat around with her muzzle and front paws until it was just the way she wanted it. Then she laid down on it and sighed as if to say "safe" and closed her eyes and slept.

This went on for a few more weeks. Ed would show up in the morning. The dog would be waiting for him outside the front door of his office. He'd open the door, feed her and talk to her for a few minutes. He would then go off to check on things and get his work done. She would curl up on the coat and go to sleep. Then when it was time for him to go home he would motion for her to go outside. She would get up and go out the door. He would tell her good night, get in his truck, and head home. He had no idea what she did at night.

One morning, she wasn't at the front door when he got to work. He looked all over for her, but finally gave up. He unlocked the

door to the office and went in. He was surprised to see the dog. He had been in a hurry
last night and had forgotten to put her out
before he left. She just stretched and walked
to the door. She went out and disappeared
into the cemetery. She was gone for about an
hour or so.

When she came back, Ed decided he
needed to know more about this dog. First,
he made a phone call. He then opened his
truck door and motioned for her to get in. At
first she just looked at him, but after a few
minutes of him motioning and patting her
on the head, she jumped in the truck. He
drove to a small building outside of town
and parked at the front of it. Opening the
door, he stepped out. She got out right behind him and followed him into the
building.

When the vet walked into the waiting
room, both Ed and the dog stood up and followed her into the exam room. After a few
minutes of checking the dog over, the vet sat
down and started talking.

"The dog is in pretty good shape, except
she is a little undernourished and she has a
few flea and tick bites. My guess is she is

about two years old. She's a little small for her breed, but healthy. I believe she is a full blooded Central Asian Shepherd."

"Never heard of them," Ed said.

"Neither had I until I went to Mongolia on a field trip four years ago. A bunch of vets went to learn about some new medicines that the Mongolians were using on their horses. While there I saw these amazing dogs that tended the goats and sheep. They also watched over the children. The people there could pretty much let their children run all over without worry. They knew that if something or someone should come by that threatened their children, the dogs would let them know something was wrong."

"So, is she a sheep-herding dog?" Ed asked.

"No. They're not a breed that herds anything. There are a lot of wolves, foxes and coyote type of predators in Mongolia. So these dogs were bred to live with the livestock. Whether it be sheep, cows, or goats, these dogs become part of the herd and protect it from any predator. They travel along with the herd. They will first sound an alarm, but if they need to, they will fight off whatever comes along. They are one-family dogs and are very protective of children. They are very rare in the states and the ones I've seen here are very expensive."

"Why would anyone spend lots of money on a dog and then just dump it?"

"Don't know. I'm guessing you've already looked for her owner."

Ed nodded his head in the affirmative.

"I do know one thing. She is very lucky to have found you. I also know she needs a bath and haircut. We have a great groomer here. I can see if he's busy."

When Ed saw the dog again, he was surprised how beautiful she looked all cleaned up. He took her out to his truck.

As he was driving back to work, he decided that he needed to give her a home. He was worried about what Joanie would say. They had had four dogs in their married life, but the boys were almost grown and gone. He and Joanie had been talking about the things they were going to do when it was just the two of them again. "Oh well, it'll be at least ten more years before I can retire. By then, this dog will probably be gone."

He and the dog returned to their routine

for the next few days while he tried to figure out how to tell Joanie he was going to bring a big dog home. As it turned out, Joanie made it easy for him. She had a surprise of her own she needed to ask Ed about.

JOANIE MET Ed at a USO dance she went to with a friend outside of Salt Lake City. She had fallen for him almost at first sight. He was a great dancer and he said he wanted a house full of kids and dogs. So did she.

After they married she studied child development in school. Joanie was a lady who loved children. She worked in schools and daycares for many years. Then one day she came home and told Ed that she wanted to work with disabled children and those that had no one in their families that could help them. She loved seeing the light go on in a child's eyes when something they were struggling with finally made sense to them.

"It makes them so happy," she'd say, "and it makes me cry."

Joanie worked with disabled children for a time. She then moved on to working with foster children. She said they got moved around so much they needed lots of extra help. She started working in a daycare that took care of foster children in the day time when their foster parents needed to work. She loved reading to them, teaching them numbers and letters, and sometimes just sitting and rocking them.

One day a little girl was brought to the day care. She was 10 months old, small, with curly blonde hair. She had a big smile when you talked to her. She was also a Down syndrome child. Joanie fell in love with her almost immediately. Her name was Amber.

AMBER WAS BORN to a young girl who didn't want her. Consequently, Amber was placed in the foster care system.

The first lady who took her in, loved her and tried to help her grow stronger and learn. But sometime in her stay with her foster mother, it was discovered that Amber had a heart defect that had to be repaired to extend her life. She had to go to the hospital for open heart surgery. By the time she healed from the surgery, the foster mom was unable to care for her. So she was given to a new foster mom.

The new foster mom didn't really want Amber, but took her because it paid well. She never did much to stimulate or motivate Amber to learn how to do new things. Most of the time, Amber sat in her car seat with nothing to play with.

When Joanie came into Amber's life at the daycare, Amber became a project. Joanie carried her around and talked to her constantly. She taught her simple sign language so she could communicate. She would place Amber on the floor so she could learn to kick her legs, move her arms and straighten her back. Joanie taught her to hold her own bottle, roll over, sit up alone and scoot around on the floor to get to what she wanted. Joanie hated sending Amber home every night with her foster Mom and always was happy to see her the next morning.

At eighteen months, Amber was now scooting all over the floor, sitting up by herself, holding her own bottle, and feeding herself small bites of food placed on her high chair tray. Then one day, Amber didn't come. Joanie asked the lady who ran the day-care where Amber was.

"I don't know," she answered. "Her case worker called this morning and said she wouldn't be coming today."

After three more days, Joanie couldn't take not knowing what was going on. She called the case worker and asked for more information. She was told that Amber's foster mom had decided she didn't want Amber anymore. She said, "The little girl was getting too mobile and hard to watch."

Amber had been sent to a new foster home. She stayed there two days. When they brought her back, they said that they just couldn't take her after all. Joanie inquired, and was told, that they were looking for a new foster home for Amber.

She thought about it for a minute, and then asked, "Would you consider me as a foster mom for Amber?"

ON THE DAY that Ed was headed home to talk to his wife about bringing a big dog home, Joanie was trying to think of a way to tell Ed that she was bringing home a new family member also, and her name was Amber.

Ed and Joanie both laughed about how it all happened. They were sitting at the kitchen table when Ed said he had something to tell Joanie. She stopped him, and asked if she could go first with her news.

After she got done telling him what she wanted to do, she said, "now it is your turn."

Ed just sat there for a minute. He then grinned and said, "Well if we are going to have a new little one around the house, don't you think that she should have a dog of her own to play with?"

Joanie cocked her head sideways and gave him a questioning look. "A dog, Ed?"

They laughed at each other being nervous to tell the other one what they wanted to do. But after the laugh, it became apparent that this was the way things were supposed to work out. They would bring both new members into the household.

The hardest part was telling their sons that there would be a new dog and little sister in their world. That took some getting used to but soon they too fell in love with the big yellow dog and the curly haired little girl.

The dog came home first. Joanie was surprised how big it was. It had a reasonably laid back personality, so it didn't bother her except the dog didn't want to stay in the sun room where her dog bed was. Ed decided to bring home the old coat she had been sleeping on at work to see if that would help. It did. As soon as he put it down on her bed she started rearranging it until it was just the way she wanted it. As Joanie watched this evening ritual of rearranging the bed, she turned to Ed and said, "Boy she sure is fussy about how she wants her bed."

Ed nodded.

"Hey," Joanie said. "That's what we'll call her—Fussy."

Thus Fussy got a new name, a new home and people who would love her and take care of her. Then it was time for Amber to be added to the family.

After all the paperwork was done the case worker brought Amber to her new foster home. All three boys, and Ed, Fussy and Joanie were there to greet her. It was a wet, cold day, so when the case worker carried Amber from the car to the house, she covered the little girl up with a large blanket.

After they were in the house and the blanket was removed, Amber started to cry. She looked scared until she saw Joanie. Then the tears dried up and she started to smile.

Joanie was concerned about how the dog and Amber would get along. Amber seemed entranced by the dog, but the dog kept out of reach of the noisy little girl. She watched Amber's every move.

One day Joanie was busy in the kitchen while Amber was playing in the family room. Amber had been trying to walk on her own for a few weeks now, but hadn't quite got the hang of it.

All of a sudden Joanie realized she hadn't heard Amber for a few minutes and it seemed quiet in the next room. She stopped what she was doing and peeked around the corner.

There were Amber and Fussy, walking together.

Amber had a handful of fur on Fussy's back. Amber would take a step, stop and let go, trying to do it on her own. But she wasn't quite ready yet and she would fall. Fussy would lie down beside her and wait until she had a good hold again. Then she would slowly stand, bringing Amber up with her. Then away they would go again.

Joanie watched this happen over and over. After that day, the two of them were rarely apart. The walking ritual went on for several weeks until one day Amber just took off on her own with Fussy following close behind. It was Amber's second birthday.

Ed came home early one day and found Joanie in the office. He left her and decided to peak in on Amber. He opened the nursery door to see if she was still asleep, but Amber was not there. He walked back to the office looking around as he went. "Joanie, where's Amber?"

"She's having her nap."

"No, she's not in her room."

Joanie took Ed by the hand and they walked together into the sun room. Ed saw Amber and Fussy curled up on Fussy's bed together.

"I found them together a few weeks ago. Amber was asleep and Fussy was covering her up with that coat. Ever since then, that's where Amber has wanted to take her nap. It looks like they were brought together by a guardian angel. They both needed a home and each other, and now they both need that old coat. Since both have claimed it, it has been a contest to see who gets it at any given moment."

Ed was watching Amber's hands. One was opening and closing on Fussy's fur. The other one was rubbing up and down on the torn silk lining of the ragged old coat. Jonnie seemed to know what he was thinking. "It seems to give her comfort. She sleeps better and longer here." After that day Fussy's bed was moved into Amber's room.

Joanie's mother loved her grandsons. But when she heard that her daughter finally had a little girl in the house she started visiting more often, always bringing gifts. Amber loved her Grandma. They'd play and laugh together for hours. And, of course, Amber loved the excitement of seeing what new things her Grandma would bring.

One day when Joanie's mother came she gave Amber a toy she had brought and told her to run off and play with it. Amber squealed with excitement and ran into the other room to play with the new toy.

Joanie's mother turned to Joanie and said, "I have something for you too." She handed Joanie a box. "I thought you might want it for Amber when she gets a little older."

As Joanie opened the box and looked at what was there, she felt shock, surprise and joy, all at the same time.

She finally reached in the box and pulled out a little girl's dress. It was pale blue with small delicate yellow flowers on it. It had a full shirt, ¾ length sleeves and a dainty rounded collar. It was buttoned down the front with six small black buttons.

"I CAN'T BELIEVE you've kept this all these years. I loved this dress, at least until we were on the ship coming to America."

"What happened on the ship?" her mother asked.

"Well, remember that lady on our ship that wore a silver fur coat no matter how hot or cold the weather was? She was watching me and two other little girls playing one day and commented on how she liked my dress.

Then she said, "Except for those black buttons. They don't match very well."

"After that I always wished I had little yellow buttons to go on it. After we got here I got two new dresses and I grew out of this dress and I forgot all about the dress and the black buttons. But now I have the resources to change the buttons to the color I want. Amber will love this dress too, I'm sure."

Her mother smiled and said "After the war when this dress was made many things were in short supply – including buttons. To fill the need, our neighbor was offered buttons from a black coat. Since it was all that was available, she used them."

When Amber was big enough to wear the dress Joanie was proven right. Amber did love it. It became one of her favorite dresses.

AMBER GREW OLDER. She learned to walk on her own. She could talk, dress herself, read numbers and letters, and recognize colors. She could play with dolls and friends, and was very opinionated about what she wanted to eat.

Fussy was there through it all. When Amber went to school, Fussy waited on the front porch until Amber's bus came up the road. The greeting between the two of them looked like they hadn't seen each other in months.

Amber learned to read and write, became part of a swim team for the disabled, and loved golfing with her Dad.

As Amber grew up, Fussy grew old. The dog spent more and more time on the old coat sleeping. Amber still loved talking to Fussy as she was getting ready for school.

When she came home after school, she also loved telling Fussy about everything that she'd done that day.

One day, Amber came to breakfast without Fussy tagging along. When Joanie asked about the dog, Amber just said that she was still in bed. After Amber left for school Joanie went into Amber's bedroom to check on the dog. She found Fussy curled up on her bed, half covered by the coat. As she reached down to pat Fussy, Joanie discovered she wasn't breathing. Fussy had died.

Joanie called Ed and told him the news. He came home at noon and began digging a large hole in the far back corner of their two acre property. It was the place Fussy sat in the shade in the summer as she watched Amber run and play all over the backyard.

They thought the hard part would be telling Amber. But that turned out to be easy. Amber had been taught about Jesus and heaven, so she seemed thrilled that her beloved dog would now be Jesus's dog.

The three of them stood over the grave that Ed had placed Fussy in and Joanie suggested they say a prayer over the grave.

Amber said a short prayer and then Ed started to shovel the dirt into the hole.

"Wait!" Amber suddenly shouted. She turned and ran to the house. Ed and Joanie looked at each other and waited. Amber soon came running out of the house with the ragged, torn, old coat. "Fussy needs her coat." She had Ed lay the coat over Fussy and then he resumed filling in the grave.

TIME PASSED AND AMBER GREW. Amber graduated from high school at the appointed time and applied for a job with a large law firm. She was accepted into the business as a mail and file clerk. She delivered files and mail for four and a half hours each morning, Monday through Friday. She was a much loved faithful employee over her twenty year career. During that time, her mother and dad both passed on to the next life.

Amber moved into a small apartment attached to her brother's home. It was small, but it worked for Amber. It had a sitting room with a small refrigerator and TV. There was a bedroom and bath adjoining it. Amber felt a little less dependent on others having her own little space.

Amber came home from golf one afternoon feeling down. Ann, Tank's wife, noticed that Amber wasn't her usual happy self.

"What's wrong?" Ann asked, as she wrapped her arms around the sad girl.

"Oh some people were calling me names today at golf."

"You've been called names before. Why is this bugging you so bad?"

"I don't know. It just is. I'm going to go shower and watch TV for a while."

"Okay," said Ann. "I'll bring some dinner in to you when it's ready." Ann brought the meal in, but Amber didn't eat very much. She acted listless and tired.

Ann suggested she could eat the rest of her meal later. "Why don't you call it a day and go to bed? We'll see you in the morning."

Amber said, "Okay."

Amber lay in bed turning over and over. She finally sighed and got up, walked over to her treasure chest and opened it. She reached in and retrieved a small, white box. She opened it and pulled out four large battered old buttons and six smaller black ones strung on a bright red piece of yarn.

Years ago the big buttons had started to fall off of Fussy's coat. Joanie was just going to chuck them in the trash but Amber had a fit and wanted to keep them. So one by one as the buttons came off, Amber saved them in the little white box that Joanie had given her to hold the six smaller black buttons that Joanie had taken off one of Amber's dresses. Ultimately all four buttons came off of the coat and ended up in Amber's treasure box. No one knew about the buttons but Amber and Joanie.

Amber loved taking them out and playing with them when she was younger. When she grew older, she strung them together on a long piece of red yarn that was left over from some craft project that her Mom had been doing. As an adult, Amber had pulled these buttons out when she was feeling bad. For some reason they seemed to give her comfort. That was what she wanted and needed tonight.

As she rolled them over and over in her hand, memories came flooding back.

They were memories of growing up in a

house with two loving parents, three brothers who adored her and a big yellow dog. Her brothers waited on her, protected her and taught her how to golf. The dog followed her everywhere. She loved talking to her, and Fussy always listened. She remembered the evening dinners that she loved. There was great food, interesting conversation, and lots of laughter.

Her brothers started to bring girlfriends to dinner. Soon some of them became wives. Before long, Amber was an aunt. She loved playing with the children, but she really loved the babies. As she was holding a new little nephew one day, she looked up at his father and said, "Babies are interesting little people aren't they."

There was her senior year in high school when she was voted Prom Queen and got to wear a beautiful dress. She danced with every boy on the basketball team. That made her feel very important. Then there was her swim team. She and her team went to the special Olympics and won two medals.

When she started work, very few people would talk to her. Many didn't think she could do the job. Amber proved them wrong. She was meticulous in her job. People soon learned that she would do well. Plus, Amber was a very happy person. She won people over as she learned their names and always said "Hi" as she delivered things.

There was a group of ladies there that got together once a month for lunch. They soon asked Amber to join them. When they found out that Amber golfed they started taking her with them golfing every week. That's where she was today when people were making fun of her.

All these memories wrapped around her like a warm fuzzy blanket and that made Amber smile. She squeezed the buttons one more time and laid them on the end table. She reached up and turned out her light, turned on her side and snuggled down under her quilt. She smiled and closed her eyes.

When Tank come home and saw that the table was set for just two, he asked about Amber.

"She had a bad day, so she just went to her room. I took dinner in to her," Ann said.

"I'll check on her later," Tank said.

As Tank entered Amber's room, the lights were out and Amber was in bed asleep.

The next morning at breakfast, again Tank asked about Amber.

"She isn't up yet," Ann said. "Let's let her sleep in. She was pretty upset yesterday."

At ten, Tank decided it was time to check in on Amber. He opened her door and walked in to see Amber still in bed. She was laying on her side, snuggled down under her quilt. Her eyes were closed and she had a smile on her face.

Tank leaned over close to her face. As he listened, he discovered she was no longer breathing.

Amber had died sometime during the night with a smile on her face.

Amber's funeral was small. It consisted of family and a few close friends. They told memories of how fun and funny she was, and all the things she had accomplished in her life.

The funeral director asked if people wanted to say their "goodbyes" before he closed the coffin. There were tears, sniffles and soft comments like, "I'll miss you" or "I love you" or "you were a very special lady."

"Okay," said the funeral director. "Are you ready?"

"Wait!" called Tank.

He walked slowly up to the front of the room and stood in front of Amber's coffin. He reached into his pocket and pulled out the battered old buttons tied together with red yarn. "I found these today as we were cleaning up your room. I don't know where they came from but I do know you loved them. I know that when you were upset, sad, mad or even sick, you'd get these buttons out and roll them around in your hand. In some odd way, they seemed to sooth you. They seemed to calm you down and relieve your stress. So when I found these I decided that you needed to have them with you during your new transition."

With tears in his eyes, he reached over and slid the buttons under Amber's hands that were folded across her chest. "I hope they bring you peace," he said.

He stepped back and nodded at the funeral director who reached up and closed the coffin. He then gently pushed it out the door to where the hearse was waiting.

AUTHOR'S NOTES

There were two experiences that motivated me to write this story. The most recent was when I read the life history of George Albert Smith, who served as President of the Church of Jesus Christ of Latter-Day Saints from May 21, 1945 to April 04, 1951.

President George Albert Smith's Coat

During his time as President, an event happened that set me to wondering "what was the impact of this simple act of human kindness." I began to wonder if President Smith's kindness made any difference in the life of this stranger. Did the man appreciate his gift? Did he keep it? What ultimately happened to the coat that was bestowed on him through inspiration and given with love for his fellow man?

The incident depicted here actually happened. The thoughts, feelings and the prayer of President Smith are the imagination of the author.

All other characters in this book are fictional. However, many of the events depicted here were actually experienced by people who lived through WWII and post WWII turmoil. These stories have been slightly altered to fit the theme of the book, but I have endeavored to keep them true to the events and feelings expressed by those who lived through them.

My Dad's Coat

The second experience happened many years ago.

For most of his life, my father was a robust man that loved life and loved his family. But in his later years, he battled cancer. He gave it a valiant fight, but finally, just before his 87th birthday, he lost the war. A few weeks after his passing, my sister, my Mother and I were going through Daddy's things. We were cleaning out his stuff. We made piles of things to go various places. There was a pile to go to the trash. There was a pile for family members, and finally a pile to be given to charity.

On the pile of things to go to charity was Daddy's nice overcoat. It was the coat he wore over his suit along with dress gloves and a white silk scarf. He always looked so distinguished when he put on his coat, wrapped his white silk scarf around his neck, and put on his gloves. As I got ready to leave, my sister asked me again if there was anything else I wanted. At first I said "No," but then on a whim, I decided to take Daddy's dress coat and take it home. Perhaps I thought I might wear it on occasion to remember him by.

As it turned out, that didn't work because it was way too big for me. It didn't fit anyone else in my family either. So, in the end, I hung it in the closet and pretty much forgot about it. From time to time I'd open the closet to get a coat and find myself looking at Daddy's coat. With a nostalgic smile, I would close the closet door and then promptly forget about it again.

It was over two years later, just after Halloween, that I had a lady from our church call me and ask if I could fill in for her and feed two young missionaries. She'd had something come up and couldn't do it. I said I enjoy having the missionaries come. So, we had two missionaries come to our home for dinner. It had been a mild fall that year. But on the day these young men came it was a cold, snowy, windy Idaho day.

As the Elders arrived, I noticed that one of the Elders had a nice warm coat on, but the other one had just a light jacket. We talked over dinner and visited about where they came from and about their successes here in this area.

When they began to put on their coats in preparation to leave, I asked the younger Elder where his coat was. I said, "You need to start wearing your heavy coat." He said the place he came from was always warm and he had never owned a heavy coat. He said he and his family hadn't had enough money to buy one before he came out.

I asked him, "How about now. It's getting cold."

His answer, "Maybe next month."

Then I suddenly remembered Daddy's

coat hanging right there in my closet. I went to the closet and took it out and said, "See if this fits you." The coat fit him perfectly, as if it was made for him!

He put his hands in the pockets and pulled out a pair of gloves and a scarf and handed them to me. I gave them back and told him that they went with the coat. I showed him how to wrap the scarf around his neck to help keep him warm.

He looked great in the coat, and best of all, he looked warm. He thanked us many times before he left. He had a big smile on his face as he walked out the door. We had never met these two missionaries before, nor did we ever see them again.

As they left, I watched them go. Looking at him from the back, I was surprised at how much he looked like my dad! I could feel tears filling my eyes. It made me miss my Dad again.

I am always amazed how the Lord takes care of those He loves, which is of course all of us. He knows not only what we need, but when we'll need it. I took the coat home a year before that young man had even heard about Christ's restored gospel or thought of going on a mission. I took the coat home without a plan for using it. I knew it would not fit me or anyone else in my family - but I took it anyway. God knew who the coat was for.

We all have opportunities in our life to tend others when they are in need of help. We just need to be prepared and willing when the occasion comes along. Often that preparation entails listening to the promptings of the Spirit, even when they don't make any sense to us.

"My name is Jehovah, I know the end from beginning; therefore my hand shall be over thee"
Abr.2:8.

ACKNOWLEDGMENTS

The author thanks the following individuals for contributions of time and support in developing and publishing this volume:

My sisters and their husbands, my children and their wives and all of My grandchildren.

My husband—without all of his support, counsel, constant encouragement and love—this book would have never materialized. I love you, Gary.

Voices that demanded to be heard inside my head in the middle of the night, causing many late hours at the computer, were:

President George Albert Smith, Brent

Cox, Isaac, Frederick, Ernst, Victor, Kurt, Thomas Grey, Ed, Joanie, Amber and Fussy.

BIBLIOGRAPHY

Teachings of Presidents of the Church: George Albert Smith Chapter 2

"A Labor of Love". By Ezra Taft Benson 1989 Publisher, Deseret Book Company

ABOUT THE AUTHOR

B. E. Clegg lives in Idaho Falls, Idaho. She is the mother of two married children and loves ten grandchildren. Elaine and her husband have shared their love and friendship for over 50 years. This book is one of four books she has authored, but is her first historically based fiction.

Contact her at gcs@gcsdistributing.com

Made in United States
Orlando, FL
23 December 2022

27586356R00088